ADDITIONAL PRAISE FOR *AN IDEAL PRESENCE*

I loved Eduardo Berti's beautifully and carefully constructed meditation on the notion of presence at death. This book left me gasping.

AMY FUSSELMAN, AUTHOR OF *IDIOPHONE & SAVAGE PARK*

Eduardo Berti's resonant homage to caretakers offers us a rare glimpse at the small moments that fill out the days of hospitals, from the humorous and warming to the unsettling and devastating. Not a word is wasted in Berti's book, nor in Daniel Levin Becker's ideal translation.

EMMA RAMADAN, TRANSLATOR & CO-OWNER OF RIFFRAFF

A magnificent book. More than the strange anecdotes that the protagonists describe, not without feeling, the atmosphere surrounding them has a quiet voice that expresses the essential: love, fear, regret, memory, illusion. There is no official language, just an internal one. With restraint and intensity, Eduardo Berti shows it by way of these simple, admirable beings who let us hear, beyond life and death, the surprising voice of truth.

SILVIA BARON-SUPERVIELLE, *LES LETTRES FRANÇAISES*

It's a tour de force to offer such emotion from such fleeting characters, and it's the opposite of a tour de force the way Berti refrains from any visible virtuosity, the apparent simplicity with which he gives body and soul to all these lives, those departing and those remaining. It's as if the reader is looked after by the hospital workers and the author at once, held in the arms of each and all. MATHIEU LINDON, *LIBÉRATION*

Each of these deaths is an unspeakable drama in itself, a little complete world snuffed out. Eduardo Berti's talent consists in making us feel the drama without adding any, by the simple multiplication of points of view. BERNARD QUIRINY, *L'OPINION*

An Ideal Presence *shows nothing but respect: for the sick at the end of life; for the medical personnel sharing their motivations, their doubts, their hesitations, satisfactions, and afflictions. How to avoid falling into pathos? What is the right distance to maintain? Eduardo Berti, who must have asked himself these questions as well, answers with a rare elegance.* MARIANNE PAYOT, *L'EXPRESS*

Curious at first, we become complicit, touched by the emotions that well up from such particular instants, from these moments that are the foundations of philosophies, beliefs, fears, religions. It's often awful, but quite beautiful sometimes too. Powerful, always. It's not macabre. It's profound. PLM, *LA VOIX DU NORD*

Also by Eduardo Berti in English

The Imagined Land

Agua

AN IDEAL PRESENCE

Fern Books
Oakland, 94609
Paris, 75020
fernfernfern.com

Copyright © Eduardo Berti
c/o Schavelzon Graham Agencia Literaria
www.schavelzongraham.com

Originally published in French as *Une présence idéale*
by Editions Flammarion, 2017

First English edition, 2020
Translation copyright © Daniel Levin Becker

ISBN: 978-1-7352973-0-9 (paperback); 978-1-7352973-1-6 (ebook)
Library of Congress Control Number: 2020944877

This is a work of fiction. Names, characters, places, and incidents are either the product of the author's imagination or used fictitiously, and any resemblance to actual persons living or dead, businesses, companies, events, or locales is entirely coincidental.

Cover art and design by James David Lee
Interior design by Kit Schluter
Logo by Helen Shewolfe Tseng
Epigraph in Lydia Davis's translation
Set in Cycles and Scala Sans

Printed in the United States

AN IDEAL PRESENCE

A NOVEL

EDUARDO BERTI

translated by Daniel Levin Becker

FERN BOOKS

OAKLAND ● PARIS

Between April and December 2015, I spent several weeks at the University Hospital Centre in the city of Rouen, France, as a guest of its palliative care department. The texts that follow were inspired, more or less freely, by what I encountered there. The names of the narrators are evidently false, as this is a work of fiction constructed out of real experience. That said, these texts are meant to pay homage to all caregivers in all palliative care units, and also to William March's book *Company K*, which inspired the form of this collection. I wish to thank the whole unit, as well as the digestive oncology unit, but also the cultural services department of the Rouen UHC and the team of the Terre de Paroles festival, who first had the idea to offer me a "medico-literary" residency in the birthplace of Gustave Flaubert, whose father was once director of the Rouen School of Medicine.

I dared to write these texts directly in French. This does not signal a change of my language of composition: I still write in Spanish and I will no doubt continue to do so, but French imposed itself here for a number of reasons, one in particular: it was in French that I discovered the universe that inspired these texts, that the earliest sentences and sketches were born.

I do not think of *An Ideal Presence* as a book about death. My intention was to write a book about life: the professional and personal lives of a group of caregivers. I wanted to understand life's place, so to speak, in a context where death is omnipresent. And, in a similar way, I wanted to understand the place of invention within a writing project such as this one, where reality and documentation are omnipresent as well. To that end, while some of the stories and characters in this book are fictional, I have remained faithful to what I saw, heard, and learned about the medical profession during my time in the UHC.

E. B.

For Jean-Marie Saint-Lu,
who is always there.

For Mariel and Ulises.

The hope of being relieved
gives him the courage to suffer.

Marcel Proust, *Swann's Way*

PAULINE JOURDAN

NURSING AIDE

No, I won't be reading your book. You've come here, I'm told, to put our work, our reality, into words. I haven't read anything of yours, I'm sorry. Perhaps I'm prejudiced. But each time I see doctors or nurses or nursing aides in a novel, in a film or on television, honestly, I want to laugh. Either it's excessive, a catalog of cheap dramas, or it's embellished, rose-colored. But it's never true. No, never. Because when they exaggerate, when they use our work to present a spectacle of human suffering, even in those cases the images are so over-the-top you'd think they were special effects. So you'll excuse me, but I'm not going to read your book. I'm afraid I won't see anything I recognize in it. That I'll discover a washed-out version of my testimony, or, worse, that I'll feel betrayed. That said, if I've agreed to speak to you, it's not only to tell you I won't be reading your book; I agreed above all because I never refuse to speak about what I do. It must be quite different for you: when a writer, an architect, a chef, a lawyer, an actor is invited to a dinner party and starts talking about his or her work, maybe people say, "Oh, how interesting!" or maybe they think, "Oh, how boring!" — but nobody ever dares to say, "Stop talking about your work, you're

ruining dinner!" Nurses and nursing aides know that's what everyone is thinking in their case. It happens to us so often that many of
us have developed the prudent habit of just staying silent. At least
outside our circle. How many of my colleagues have you spoken
to? Have they told you about the funeral makeup, the vomit, the
cleaning tasks of hospital workers? Are you going to describe all of
that? Are you going to ruin the reader's dinner? Really? I'm asking
because I won't read you, no matter how you answer.

MARIE MAHOUX

NURSE

That lady was somebody special. I'm not saying that because she was my first patient. I'm saying it because she really was special. A very sensitive woman. Serene. And extraordinarily kind — luckily for me, because I had just arrived in the palliative care unit straight out of nursing school. A very unusual career path, I know; in theory, you go through other services first. But that wasn't the case for me. I came to the unit very young. I was barely twenty-two.

It was my fifth day in palliative care. I was still finding my footing when a patient died. That's part of the routine. We have about a hundred deaths here every year. I really mean a hundred — that's not a metaphor, it's one death every three days, roughly. But this was my first death. No, of course it wasn't my fault. I say "my" death, which I feel I can say because he passed away right in front of me, just like that, like a leaf falling from a tree. He was in his sixties and his lungs were ruined, gone up in smoke along with his chances of survival.

I didn't want to cry, but I felt the need to close my eyes, to hold my breath and count: one, two, three, four... up to twenty. After that I called Clémence, Sylvie, and Pauline, who were on the afternoon rotation with me. When they saw my face, they suggested I go out for a minute to get some air, to think about something else. They'd take care of it. I was grateful, and at the same time a bit hurt. But I did what they said. I went down the stairs and drank a coffee, standing up, facing the coffee machine. The plastic cup trembling in my hands.

Ten minutes later, Clémence sent me on my rounds to the eleven other rooms. They didn't want me to see the body again, that was clear. I didn't take the usual route. I left that special woman—my first patient—for last. I remember thinking as I was making my rounds that I was the only one in the whole unit to have my first patient still in the hospital. I remember thinking also, with a pang of sadness, that soon I would be like everyone else...

I had kept my first patient for last because I thought she would calm me down. She always seemed so serene. Like she thought it was totally logical and ordinary to be there, in her bed. She had barely seen me come into the room when she opened her eyes wide.

"Did something happen, my dear?"

(That's what she called me: "my dear.")

I barely managed to smile and answer:

"No. Nothing at all."

"Come now... there's been a death, hasn't there?" she asked.

I was dumbstruck for a moment.

"How do you know?"

"You can just feel it, my dear. You can feel it in the air."

CAMILLE ZIRNHELD

NURSING AIDE

Late one afternoon, a Friday, I was with my partner, Awa, and another pair was also on duty: Morgane and Solène, I think. That's how we work here. You've already been told all that, I assume. A nurse and a nursing aide, in tandem. Anyway, it was Friday, as I was saying, and I knew I had the weekend off, that neither Awa nor I would be back at work until Monday, so I took the piece of paper where I usually note down—like a checklist for myself—the names of the twelve patients and each one's room number, and then, all of a sudden, without quite knowing why, I underlined eight names and said, just like that, quickly, in front of my three coworkers: "The other four, they won't be here on Monday." I meant, obviously, the patients whose names I hadn't underlined.

I had forgotten all of this by Monday, when Solène saw me come in and told me an awful and strange thing: my prediction had come true.

Everyone was looking at me, wondering how I could have known. Of course I hadn't known anything. I'd just guessed. It's crazy. I'd guessed. Now I was rattled. And mortified. Needless to say, I've never done anything like that again. Not even for myself, in secret. No, never.

HÉLÈNE DAMPIERRE

NURSE

I'm in the middle of a conversation with him, talking freely. Since he arrived here two weeks ago, it's already become a routine: we talk about this and that, about life in general. And then, without meaning to, just totally naturally, I use the informal *toi* with him. Right away I want to backpedal — but how? I know I've crossed the line. And yet he seems delighted: he wants to be informal with me too. And it becomes the custom between us. All the same, I mention it to Madame Terwilliger. "What's done is done, Hélène," she tells me. It's too late now. These things happen. And after all why not? Still, in the days that follow, I can tell it's created an imbalance with my coworkers. I'm the only one he uses *toi* with.

A week later, during an ordinary conversation, he lets slip: "It's nice to be informal with each other. But I advise you not to become my friend, because soon you're going to lose me." He says the words calmly. With a serene anger. With a mix of bitterness and resignation. And I stay there, speechless. If there's one thing you learn quickly in this line of work, it's to keep quiet when there's really no way to answer.

CATHERINE KOUTSOS

RESIDENT

There were six or seven of us around the bed when Patricia Long walked into the room.

"Madame," Patricia began, her voice trembling slightly because she knew the importance of what she was about to say. "Madame, it's your oldest son. He's here to see you."

Everyone in the unit knew the story. Mother and son hadn't spoken in ten years. The old woman, a widow, regularly received visits from a sister, older than her, and also from a very shy niece who never said more than a word or two. The son's absence was more powerful than the presence—overly discreet, almost invisible—of those two women.

"Madame," Patricia pressed. "Your son... in the family room."

We were in the middle of the woman's physical exam. Two nurses, two nursing aides, two externs, and me, the only resident.

The lady, who had her eyes closed while we were examining her, opened them with rage and responded simply:

"No, no."

"You don't want to see him?" asked Jacqueline Marro with a slight note of surprise.

"No, no," repeated the woman.

And she added, with resentment:

"Of course not! He has no business here. You tell him to leave, please."

I stared at the woman. Should we push the point, or just respect her wishes? When I looked away, I saw seven pairs of eyes fixed on me. By a sort of tacit accord, everyone had decided it was me who would go speak to the son.

I'm used to delivering terrible news to people: "You have leukemia," "I'm afraid you only have five or six months left to live"... Not that it doesn't affect me. But humans have a way of getting used to astonishing things. And yet, for all my experience, my palms were all clammy, like the first time I had to tell a patient he had an incurable disease.

The son was waiting, standing in the entrance to the family room. My body and my facial expression must have told him enough, because he extended his hand and asked me directly: "She doesn't want to see me, right?" He made it easier for me. I answered, "No, no..." And while saying it, without wanting to, I imitated, just a bit, the way his mother had said it. He thanked me, smiled sadly. He was about to leave when he came back toward me.

"Could I see another room, at least?"

Surprised, I asked if he meant he wanted to see another patient. But no, he just wanted to visit another room. To get a sense of the place where his mother would no doubt die?

There were no empty rooms. That's quite rare here, you know. But there was a room whose patient had gone off for a chemo session.

"Alright," I said.

A few seconds later we were both in the room across from his mother's. I felt like a real estate agent waiting for the client to finish his walkthrough. Finally, he murmured:

"Okay, I see. Yes, okay."

I walked the son out. He held out his hand to me a second time. It was even sweatier than mine. He never came back to see his mother. I still remember his last look. It was the unhappy look of a child who has been unfairly punished.

AWA MODOU
NURSE

It was Virginie, a coworker from the department where I worked before, who gave me the idea. "It's perfect for you," Virginie insisted. "You have a spiritual side, you know how to listen to patients, you're not afraid of death." I wasn't convinced. Of course I'm afraid of death. At the same time, it's true, I like testing limits. *My* limits. I worked in a retirement home for almost two years. And for more than a year in a psychiatric hospital. At the very beginning, when I was a visiting nurse, I accepted a job nobody in my cohort wanted: caring for a very sick man with no family who was going to die at home. The man was nice, but in a terrible state, plus he refused my help washing himself. It was a two-week exercise in patience. Eventually the man allowed me to bathe him. He died a few hours later.

I had been sort of unsatisfied recently. I'd even thought about changing jobs when Virginie told me about the palliative care unit, where her sister Hélène had been working for a while. I'd heard, of course, that palliative care received patients with serious, chronic, terminal diseases. I knew the objective of the unit was not only to ease physical pain but also to attend to emotional suffering, to be there for the loved ones. I knew all of this — I had even written it out in blue ink, almost seven years prior, for an exam on which I did relatively well.

I talked about it with Hélène, Virginie's sister. Like me, she knew that in other sectors of the hospital, if a nurse takes care of twelve or fourteen beds, she can't spend more than fifteen to twenty minutes a day with each patient. "We, on the other hand, manage to spend almost an hour with them," Hélène explained, though she made it clear that you also had to be ready for extreme situations.

I applied. The palliative care unit gave me an appointment, and I had an hour-and-a-half interview with Madame Gosselin, the head of the unit. Madame Gosselin told me everything, showed me everything: twelve single rooms, twelve beds total, night shift from 8:30 p.m. to 6:30 a.m., morning shift from 6:10 a.m. to 1:51 p.m., afternoon shift from 1:10 p.m. to 8:45 p.m., a room with a huge bathtub which Madame Gosselin likes to joke is the luxury reward for the best patients, a staff of a dozen nursing aides and a dozen nurses. All the while she asked me questions: what does pain mean to me, what does it mean to care for a patient. And, above all, why this unit.

"I don't want to work without my values, without taking the human into account," I told her straight out. I hadn't prepared these words, or any kind of speech. I promise you. I remember this sentence coming out of my mouth like someone else had said it before me. I say it to myself now, sometimes, like a proverb. "I don't want to work without my values." That's it.

JOSÉPHINE BOULLEAU

MOBILE UNIT NURSE

Two years ago, after five years as a nurse in the palliative care unit, I was invited to move to the mobile unit, a sort of extramural extension of our service. The members of this unit are supposed to provide "offsite" care, but that's a vast concept: sometimes it means walking down the twenty steps to the pneumology section on the lower level of our building; sometimes it means getting in the Twingo and driving an hour and a half to see a single patient in a village whose name you won't remember three days later. I've had to go out on my own, or with a doctor or the young psychiatrist, Mélanie Lemaire, or even sometimes with both. Last week, for example, I went with Marie-France Bergeret to see the family of a man with a serious disease. We arrived at the retirement home more than a hundred kilometers away, only to find nobody there. A miscommunication...

In the mobile unit I had one of the most memorable experiences of my life. The emergency service had called me to see a patient. It was eleven at night and the man had just arrived at the hospital. Someone had found him half-conscious in the street. As soon as I saw him, I knew he was going to die. It was a matter of minutes. After so many years in palliative care, you can see it immediately. The emergency personnel hadn't called the family yet (he was married, but I didn't know that until later), we had to look through his papers—which takes time—and most of all, may I add, nobody had realized he was so close to the end. The man was living out his last minutes alone, and I felt like I had to stay with him. He shouldn't die all alone, even if he was already almost unconscious.

It's odd, staying next to a stranger to escort him into death. Dying is an intimate act. And yet I couldn't leave. I took his hand. That way he would know there was someone by his side... He turned his back to me, he kept his eyes closed, he was barely moving anymore. But his hand held my hand, and he could—why not—attach to my touch whatever face he wanted.

Suddenly, I could feel he no longer wanted me there. I took my hand back, gently. He began to groan. It was painful. It was over.

I stayed in the room. I waited for his wife to arrive; they had just told me they'd called her. She would show up soon, and I could tell her about her husband's death. But I was already being called again. I couldn't stay. I asked the emergency doctor if he could give the wife my number. Not my personal number, but the mobile unit's. That way she could get in touch with me and I could at least tell her that her husband had passed peacefully enough, that he hadn't suffered too much.

I spent the rest of the day in quite a state. I kept seeing the man's last moments. I was imagining not only what I would say to his wife, but also how I'd present the facts. I built a detailed story in my head, chose my words, perhaps too carefully, constructed an embellished version of this poor man's death. I was rather satisfied with the words I had prepared. I was ready and anxious, as if the man were still suffering, as if he were waiting to finish dying until the exact moment his death, the story of his death, left my mouth and reached his wife's ears.

Can you believe it? The wife never called. Not that day, not in the days after. So I took a notebook and I wrote down, sentence by sentence, my nice little speech. Alas, once it was written, once it was set down in the notebook, it seemed very disappointing, much less powerful than it had been in my head. I guess you must know that feeling, being a writer. I kept the notebook in a drawer and finally, over time, forgot about it. I only found it again a few months ago. But I couldn't bring myself to reread it, no. It's the story of someone else's death... Honestly, I think I should burn that notebook. Like a sort of cremation. A burial. I don't know. Nor do I know whether I'll have the courage to go through with it.

PASCALE RAMBERT

DOCTOR

People avoid each other in the family room. They do it under the pretext, which isn't all that false, of not bothering others. They do it most of all, in truth, because their own pain is enough for them.

NADIA CHOUNIER

NURSE

I won't say his name, out of respect for doctor-patient confiden-
tiality, but also because his name is still painful to me, in spite of
the time that's gone by. He was young. He was barely a year older
than me. He was single—he had some friends his age who came to
visit him, most of them with a family, a wife and kids, and I could
see he was delighted to see them, but that for him family life was
an unrealized dream... what do they call it? A missed opportunity,
that's it.

He was very weak from the pain. He was somewhere else more
and more of the time, because of the opioids we administered to
calm him down. One day, however, he did an astonishing thing.
He sent one of his best friends out to buy a bouquet of flowers. For
me. The friend came into the room with the bouquet and gave it
to him. He struggled to take it in his big hands, which had started
trembling. A few minutes later, he held it out to me without saying
a word. I had had a hard year. A breakup. My self-esteem wounded
by falling out of love. Those flowers, I'll never forget them. I know:
he, the patient, was, in a sense, paradoxically enough, taking care
of the nurse.

He was very shy, very respectful. However, one day while another one of his friends was there, he ventured, "Hey, this is Nadia. I wanted you to meet her. She doesn't know it yet, but I'm in love with her. I should have met her a bit earlier, it's a pity." I blushed like a schoolgirl. I couldn't tell you what I said, but I made him understand how touched I was by his words. And from that moment on, we made a little joke of the whole thing. He teased me in front of everyone. I was "his fiancée," "his girlfriend." We laughed. Of course, I kept my distance. But at the same time, I never stopped thinking of his words: "I should have met her a bit earlier, it's a pity." Yes, it was truly a pity.

DANIÈLE POURCELY
NURSING AIDE

I had just arrived in the unit and a nurse was retiring. They had put together a going-away party. Someone had brought in a few bottles of champagne. We don't drink on the job. Except when it's a patient's birthday and the family comes with a bottle. In that case we're often invited to join, and the custom is to accept and take a tiny sip, nothing more. But that day, this nurse was drinking. It was her last day and she was overwhelmed.

We were in our kitchen and suddenly she handed me a glass and started telling me about a patient she had known at the beginning of her career, in the 1980s. The man was old, nothing left but skin and bones. He didn't speak to anyone. He seemed indifferent to everything. She felt invisible to him. Nonetheless, one morning when she was alone with him in his room, she heard the bed creak and the old man's voice asking her very politely if she could show him her breasts. At first she thought it was a joke. She was going to laugh, but suddenly she thought better of it, maybe he was delirious, maybe it was an extravagance caused by the morphine. So she took the precaution of not saying anything. She acted as though for once it was him, the patient, who was invisible.

The next day, though, the man tried again. She just responded by shaking her head. But the man was obstinate. "In two weeks I'll be gone. This is all I ask of you. You're the youngest one here. The prettiest. The sweetest. The only one who's not married, if I'm not mistaken." No, indeed, he was not mistaken. But the idea was scandalous. Who did he take her for? "I'm sorry, but I don't think that would be right," she said. The man insisted, still with the same arguments. "You're not like the others. You're extraordinary." She saw him there, in his bed. He had a pleasing way of smiling. And his voice, above all, his voice was seductive. No doubt he had been a handsome man.

Back then she was still living with her parents. Naturally, she didn't tell them anything about all this. But the man was indefatigable. "The two breasts, please. Or at least one breast." One day she thought, why not? The man was going to die soon. The fleeting vision of a breast was an easy charity to give him. An insignificant thing compared to his suffering. It would remain between her and him. And, after the old man's death, it would remain in her mind as an amusing memory in a series of rather morbid memories. She decided to do it, and said to herself: "The ideal time to do it is the day after tomorrow, Thursday, when I'll be on the night shift. There won't be many people around, and nobody will see us."

The man died the next day, a day before. Perhaps it was for the best. She wasn't very religious, but she couldn't help thinking that God wanted it this way. A week later, during a coffee break, another nurse confided in her that that man who had just died had asked her to undo her hair and show him her thighs. He had used a thousand arguments to try to convince her: "You're so pretty, you're so unique..." She never found out whether this nurse had acquiesced to the patient's wishes.

Today, she said, she suspected the man had asked the same thing of all her colleagues. All told, even if she hadn't had time to accept his proposition (even if she had perhaps been the only one not to go all the way with it, she exaggerated three decades later), it was still a funny memory. The perfect memory to share on the occasion of her last day of work.

You'll see, later on. When you've worked nonstop all your life. When, what's more, you liked your work. When you still feel young. That's when retirement is dangerous. You have to figure out quickly how to spend your time. Me, I was a schoolteacher and also did some acting. The daughter of a good friend, a doctor here at the UHC, told me one day about something they were setting up: volunteers to come read to patients. They wanted to build a team of two or three people. The project has been going for a year, but for the moment the team of readers is just me. I'm here two mornings a week. At first I came in the afternoon. But I noticed that in the morning the patients are more receptive and have fewer visitors. It's better. In my backpack, at the UHC, I have about a dozen books, mostly story collections. Personally I prefer novels. Reading a short story, I often say, is like visiting a place; reading a novel is like living there. Yes, I can see you don't fully agree. Anyway, stories, given their length, are ideal to read out loud to patients. I always have Chekhov and Maupassant with me. I knock on the door, if it's not open. I introduce myself, because, you know, the patients change constantly here. Sometimes I have to introduce myself more than once because the oldest patients tend to forget everything.

Some patients ask for a particular author or genre. One Tuesday morning, a lady asked me to come back that Thursday with an erotic novel. I went to my neighborhood bookstore, where I often chat with the owner. He suggested two or three novels, each steamier than the last. I came back on Thursday with my book, and the woman was ecstatic. She said, "We're not going to read it all, right? Let's go straight to the good parts." The author wasn't much of a stylist, but he had his talents, his charm. The problem was that the woman would burst out laughing every time there was a slightly suggestive passage. It was hard for me to keep reading.

A week or two later, for the first time, another woman, younger but more withered by illness, asked me to read her a whole novel. Madame Mathilde, as everyone called her, wanted a detective novel. "A good detective novel, something by Simenon, if that's okay with you?" she asked, as if it were up to me to decide. I went back to see her a week later with a Simenon novel. I had planned out, in my head, seven or eight reading sessions. At first everything went well. Even if she was getting steadily weaker, even if she sometimes seemed to nod off, lulled by the rhythm of the text, it didn't matter, she followed without difficulty. The proof was that as soon as I walked into her room she would start talking to me about the possible solutions to this mystery that had gotten under her skin.

There were only two or three chapters left when Madame Mathilde's state took a swift turn for the worse. We had to cancel our reading session three times in a row because she was in too much pain, physically almost unrecognizable. A nursing aide to whom I said as much told me this happened often, that it was always a bad sign. The experience I've gathered since confirms this. But this woman wanted to know at all costs how the book ended. To the point that one day, a Wednesday, I got a call from the hospital. It was Jacqueline Marro, if I remember correctly.

"I know you normally only come on Tuesdays and Thursdays, but Madame Mathilde woke up today a bit more lucid and is asking for you. She wants to finish the novel."

An hour later I was here. I said hello to Madame Mathilde, who fluttered her eyelids, nothing more. She seemed truly fragile, but also fully present.

I began reading the last pages of the novel. I sensed that she was summoning all the strength she had left to stay with the story.

After half an hour, I looked up. It was getting late, and I had to stop reading in order to turn on a light. I looked Madame Mathilde in her eyes and said: "Not much longer."

I paused, flipped through the book.

"Thirty pages and we're done."

At that moment I saw that her eyes were open wide, cold and lifeless.

I called Jacqueline, who came running. Yes, Madame Mathilde had just died. I was shaken. I couldn't leave the room or get up from my chair. So, Jacqueline and I, we agreed: I would finish reading the novel. Out loud. While she tidied Madame Mathilde's things.

I don't remember anything about the book's plot. But I remember the chill I felt when Jacqueline closed Madame Mathilde's eyes. I remember, also, that the emotion didn't take my breath away. That I eventually made it to the last page. And that the last word in the book was not *death*, no. But a word one letter shorter: *life*.

JACQUELINE MARRO

NURSE

I woke up in the emergency room. I could barely tell where I was (in what section of the UHC, I mean), I had a vague memory of my last thoughts before my fall, and I had no idea how much time had passed. I remembered, on the other hand, the moment I had felt my legs buckle. The world had spun; I had the innocent thought, for just a second, that it was an earthquake. A nurse explained to me that Delphine Ziegler had found me passed out, at the foot of Madame Doubouloz's bed. Poor Madame Doubouloz, whom I'd just been talking to about who knows what so I didn't have to tell her her face looked completely disfigured by pain, the poor woman had rung her alarm and shouted sharply: "She's dead! Jacqueline is dead!" All of which set off, naturally, a chain reaction. All of the patients were frightened, without exception. Half an hour later, Delphine Ziegler showed up at my bed. She had told everyone she was going to smoke a cigarette in the courtyard. But she actually wanted to check on me. Before leaving again, she told me I had made a hell of an impression on Madame Doubouloz. I may not have been dead, but I had fainted after seeing her: her face was so awful, so terrifying, that she made everyone swoon, including the nurses. I wanted to break the doctors' orders and go to the palliative care unit to reassure the patients. Not an option. I was to rest. They were going to run some tests. I managed to call Richard and explain everything to him. "I'm coming," he answered. "I'm getting in a taxi right now." When he arrived at my bedside, I had just learned that I was pregnant.

CARINE LE BRUN

NURSING AIDE

Some people, like me, prefer to work at night. So we do it regularly. For instance, you've already spoken to Hélène, right? She's often paired with me. She'll tell you it's calm at night. But it's also scarier than the day. You can hear the patients' breathing more clearly, their moans of pain, the mechanical sounds of the machines, the words being exchanged, the silences. Working at night is a little like living in reverse. The downside is social isolation. Living in a world where all your friends are asleep when you have the time and desire to see them. Taking turns sleeping in bed, when you're in a couple… like the story about the poor laborers who share a mattress, you know? That's why, from time to time, you have to ask people who aren't night-shift specialists to come lend a hand.

There are rules at night: no more than two visitors per room. Only one of the two visitors gets a small cot. We had to make these rules after one night where four people slept around the same patient and it was impossible to work, to care for him or even move. The hardest moment of the night is bedtime, just before sleep. The window between 9 p.m. and midnight. Sometimes a patient will call and ask, in a child's voice, "Leave the door open a bit, please." That's not a good sign. No, never.

VALÉRIE LE PANNO

NURSING AIDE

They couldn't make up their minds. Some members of the family agreed that it was better for her to stay in the hospital. Others thought she should go home. Each thought his or her option was the safer one. As for the patient, she was divided between the two possibilities. Our psychiatrist came in and suggested a "leave," which in this case meant a two-day release with one overnight at home. Everyone thought the leave would help the family make a decision. But after the leave nothing seemed to have changed.

It's easy enough to understand their doubts: our unit is, especially for the sickest patients, a bit like a cocoon. Some patients jokingly say it's a "five-star" place, in terms of comfort and service. One day, coming from a unit where the doors are a reddish orange, a patient told me he had just crossed through the gates of hell. Three days later he amended his judgment slightly: "A five-star hell."

But to get back to this woman: even the nursing aides and nurses, we had differing opinions. One day she asked me, "What's best for me, Valérie? Should I stay here or go back home?" "Go home," I answered, at the exact moment that Charlotte, coming into the room behind me, blurted out, "Stay here."

The hardest thing, for me, is seeing children of four, five, six in the hallway. Especially when the patient is their father or their mother. You've seen little Léa, I imagine. Her mother has been in the unit for three weeks. Her father or her aunt goes to pick her up from school. She comes here for a little while before going home. She stays longer on the weekends. In the room with a TV and some children's books, the piano, the sofa, the table, and the kitchenette. I help her a bit with her homework sometimes. I have a daughter her age. It's easy — no, easy isn't the word. It's very hard, as I said before, but paradoxically it also helps to have a child here. Children keep us from getting depressed. We can't just stop. They're the life that goes on.

This morning, going from Léa's mother's room to the staff lounge, I see that the little girl seems sadder than usual, almost distraught. So I quickly think up a little speech. I breathe deep. I kneel down in front of her and let my words out, telling myself the whole time that above all I have to listen to her. Soon Léa explains to me that she's sad because her teddy bear has a long stain on its belly. A bloodstain, Léa says. A chocolate stain, explains her father, who's sitting next to her. The teddy bear, dirty and stinky, sets the whole unit in motion. As if it were a desperate case. Emergency cleanup. Fragile object. A few minutes later the bear comes out of the dryer, emerging from behind the porthole window like some kind of astronaut. It's still warm when I place it into Léa's hands.

"Is that better, like that?"

"Yes," the little girl says to me. Her eyes are shining. "He's cured!"

CLÉMENCE LE MAY

NURSE

The older sister of the husband of this patient—a woman with a strong personality—came to ask us not to tell her sister-in-law the whole truth, because her condition had just deteriorated again. It was Noémie who spoke to her at first, quietly. But I heard their conversation and I went over. Noémie was trying to explain that you don't lie to them, ever. And that this isn't purely an ethical position. That above all it's a practical one.

"In fact, madame," Noémie said to her, "patients always sense the truth. Even the ones who pretend to not want to know. The major problem is usually at the end, when the patient detects the lie and turns inward, overwhelmed by the information that's just fallen on his head, out of the blue. And worst of all is the lack of trust after the truth is discovered. No, no, you never lie. Embellish the truth a bit, fine... but nothing more."

The woman simply said: "Yes, I see."

But this woman had the lying bug, so to speak, and she went to tell her brother that we had treated her poorly. That we had intentionally given her incorrect information. Over time, you realize that this kind of thing happens fairly often: a misdirected anger, aimed at the caretakers, as though it were our own fault. Which is, ultimately, another way of lying to oneself.

MORGANE BRUCKNER

NURSE

I was seven or eight, I think, when I first became aware of sickness and suffering. I was keeping my grandmother company, and she was very sick. My parents had entrusted me with this task. I spent almost two years by her bedside. I discovered that I had a knack for this work. It was my grandmother who told me one night, "My dear Morgane, you know what? You'd make an excellent nurse!"

If you talk to the other girls on the unit, if you talk to the other nurses in the hospital in general, you'll quickly see that two stories are more or less recurring: girls who, like me, had to take close care of a sick person at home, and girls who have a nurse in the family, for instance a mother, who passed the vocation down to them.

When I'm tired, when a case turns out to be complicated, when personal troubles interfere with my work, I say to myself: "Morgane, this is your grandmother in this bed. Go ahead, show her that she was right. That you're an excellent nurse."

I am, along with Marianne Soulier, one of two medical secretaries. It's the job most removed from the patients, I won't deny it. And yet I know everything about them, because one of my main jobs is to write or help write the reports that the doctors and the internists file. I know everything from a strictly medical point of view, but usually I know nothing about the patients' physical appearance. Of course, I could stop in and see them, I could walk into the rooms and take a quick look. But, to be honest with you, I don't like to. I like to walk down the hall that leads to the rooms, so I don't lose sight of what the caretakers do; so that the smell of disease, which is more intense the closer you get to the beds, gives my work a greater sense of urgency. But entering the rooms... no, I don't think it's my place to do that.

Marianne, the other secretary, does it from time to time. It's easy to do, and if you want to you can always find a reason to justify your presence. Me, no, I prefer to just imagine the patients. It's very strange, though: some patients resist my imagination... and, on the contrary, there are some I can conjure, so to speak, completely. It's like when you read a book, a novel. You can picture certain characters perfectly, and not necessarily because the writer has given you a long and scrupulous description of them—and others, conversely, you can't. It's a mystery, I think.

At first, three years ago, when I started working in the unit, Marianne said things to me like "Ah, Monsieur Whatsit, yes, a very thin man, blond, in his fifties..." and she wouldn't stop until she'd described him from head to toe. In time I managed to explain to her that no, I didn't want to hear these little portraits, that I prefer to imagine the patients for myself... plus, that way, we're even, since they don't know me either. Go ask them what the old medical secretary looks like! We could have some fun with the imagined portraits they'd make of me, don't you think?

PATRICIA LONG

NURSING AIDE

He was a man who complained constantly. An unpleasant, disagreeable man, from what I've heard, but who are we to judge people that way? What will we be like on our deathbeds? I told myself I had to see him with my own eyes. And yes, it was true. He wasn't an easy man to be around. Not at all. He was someone used to giving orders, someone who had been powerful and now couldn't bear his impotence, in the ordinary sense of the word. Someone who, out of arrogance, didn't want anyone to see that he was petrified with fear.

Bizarrely, he was very polite with me. Maybe because I talked to him sweetly. Maybe because I found a way to make it seem like he was giving me orders. Superficial orders, obviously, and simple to accomplish. But it did him good, and it was so easy for me to arrange.

My colleagues continued to speak of him reproachfully. It was a bit unfair, but at the same time I understood — it was enough to hear him protest whatever they were doing. Even his family had a hard time putting up with his bad moods.

One day I sensed a nervous energy in him. He wouldn't stop giving me orders: go fetch some water, or throw the water in the toilet because it tasted strange. Raise his bed, or lower it.

"Can you close the door and come here for a moment, please?" he asked me at last.

As a rule, I always have a colleague with me in front of patients. And I certainly don't close the door if I find myself alone with one of them. You never know, you can't be too careful. But our entire relationship was on the line here, I felt: if I showed him I didn't trust him, if I showed him I was afraid to close that door and hear what he was going to say to me, I would no longer be able to look him in the face.

I thought: I'll obey. And I approached him with all the serenity I could feign.

"Thank you," he told me then, in a whisper-thin voice. "Thank you for giving me my dignity back."

SYLVIE COMPÈRE

DOCTOR

Relations between doctors and caregiving personnel can be tense. Doctors criticize nurses and nursing aides for being too emotional; they criticize us, on the other hand, for being too impersonal. It's true that some doctors will say "I'll be back, I've got to go see a pancreas," that they don't see the whole person, only the sick parts — the pathology. Obviously you can't generalize. You'll find all types: doctors convinced of the accuracy of what is in my opinion a disgusting metaphor (that they're the brain of the unit and that the nurses and nursing aides are the arms and heart), nurses who think they know more than us, etc. There is ultimately a great misunderstanding that comes from a false perception: nurses can spend an hour a day with each patient; we spend barely ten or fifteen minutes with them, because we have other things to do. Things that also affect the patients, but this relative invisibility leads some nurses to think that we don't care very much, that we're less engaged than they are.

Things are better these days. Twenty years ago, when I started working in hospitals, I had some rather aggressive experiences. I spent a few years at a hospital in Lille where there was a rumor that the doctors were taking bets on the health of certain patients. Bets for money, I mean. Bets about their date and time of death, for instance. And that they were wagering astronomical amounts. This was false, complete nonsense. But the rumor blew up so much that a tabloid published a little article on the subject. The article went so far as to imagine that a doctor could hasten the death of a patient in order to win a bet or help one of his friends win... hell of a get-rich-quick scheme! The older doctors got quite angry and claimed the nurses had started the rumor. Me, I don't believe so. It was an urban legend, as they say. That gives you a good idea of the situation.

I get an urgent call from the new patient in room 6. As soon as I open the door, the woman begins to bark:

"You're just a nursing aide! I demand to see a nurse! And I know you're not even a nursing aide, just an intern! No, no!"

Some people believe strongly in hierarchy. People who start to look, the moment they arrive, for a hierarchical code on our scrubs: the color yellow for the nursing aides, the color green for the nurses, the color blue for support staff... All told, it's a good sign when they get worked up, when they manage to express their feelings. Much better, you know, than fatalism and resignation.

NOÉMIE SAINT-ANDRÉ

NURSING AIDE

The worst thing you can do is talk about them like they're not there. I've seen doctors, nurses, and relatives do it. Once, a family was speaking in raised voices in front of the patient. They were planning their Christmas dinner. A meal the patient wouldn't be going to, obviously, because he would be spending Christmas at the hospital. On December 26th, coming back from a two-day break, when Marie Mahoux told me that the patient had passed away the night of the 24th at eleven o'clock exactly, I wasn't surprised at all.

Other families do exactly the opposite: they don't talk about anything in front of the patient. As though the slightest comment could hurt him, distress him. It's the other extreme. An excess of protection. In that case, over the silence, the patient begins to fantasize.

I remember one old man, very nice and very clever: Monsieur Pascal. Everyone told him, "Come on, Monsieur Pascal, you're just fine the whole day, and then as soon as your family arrives you fall asleep!" He would laugh. He wouldn't say anything, he'd just laugh. I quickly understood what he was up to. When his wife and his son thought Monsieur Pascal was sleeping, they whispered things that they normally hid from him. That way he got all the information he wanted.

Ah, I can still see Monsieur Pascal's face as he slept. What an actor. The day he died, I wondered if he wasn't just playing another trick on us.

ANNE-LAURE BELMONT

DOCTOR

From experience, I dare say most of the people who work in the unit are opposed to euthanasia. In my view, people ask to die mainly because they can't deal with great physical suffering. But once the physical suffering is relieved, the request disappears... I've seen this even in cases where the patient is confined to his bed. It's interesting. Contrary to certain received ideas, it's not death that creates suffering; it's suffering that creates the desire or the need to die.

This morning Joséphine and I went a few kilometers away to visit an old woman, ninety-nine years old. It's funny to say, but she doesn't look ninety-nine. She seems much younger... let's say eighty-two or eighty-three. I don't know. After eighty, I have a hard time estimating ages.

In spite of her healthy appearance, this woman no longer wants to eat, no longer wants to take medicine or sedatives. She's tired of everything: of her body, of her pain, of seeing her family waste time at her bedside. "I'm even tired of the sunrise," she told us. But her children and grandchildren don't agree: they want to have someone in their family reach a hundred. It would be a pity, as they see it, to fall short by so little.

There's a bit of egotism in all this, to be sure. But at base, there's something inspiring in it, a little bit of affectionate bait to spur on the almost-hundred-year-old.

The lady will turn one hundred in four months, in October. Four months—a trifle for you, for me, for her children and her grandchildren. For her, though, it's like crossing the desert. She told me this in confidence, furrowing her eyebrows: "I can't do it."

And she added, "The idea of being a hundred horrifies me." And then she let out a bitter laugh, while we gave her a sedative injection and Josephine spoke with her family. Just then I remembered that I had bought train tickets this morning for a trip my husband and I are taking in December. And such a simple thing struck me as obscene.

The patients don't always know there's a beautician available
to them. One or two of the girls do publicity for me. Mostly Clémence. She's in the habit of saying to patients, "Don't hesitate to
call Suzanne, if you want to look a little better." Behind this joke,
there's a legitimate desire on the patients' part to present a more
dignified image.

I came to the unit by chance, after I saw an ad in the paper. I
thought it was a joke, a bit like those Pierre Dac ads, do you know
those? "Student seeks painter to help brush up his algebra," that
sort of thing.

I had a long interview. They explained all the unit's particular-
ities to me. I said yes, yes, I'll stay here, I'll work here. I do mani-
cures. I do facial massages. I do makeup only if the patients have
their own makeup with them, because I don't have the necessary
products with me. The hardest thing, at first, was getting used
to the posture of bedridden and sometimes feeble bodies. I was
taught to do my job just one way: standing behind my clients, at
a certain height and a certain distance. I had to get used to more
contorted positions.

Today, after seven years, I don't think I could go back to work, in a beauty salon somewhere. Here I don't have to sell anything. No products, no treatments. I can devote my time to doing good work.

Last Tuesday, for instance, I made up a woman who wanted to get married to her companion. I spent almost an hour beautifying her. And I think it was one of the finest makeup jobs of my career. To the point that I wondered if she was going to invite me to stay for the private ceremony in her room. A deputy mayor, witnesses, friends, and family would be there. A dozen people, no more. I knew the woman and her husband had thought to ask a member of the team to represent the unit, but because they didn't want to hurt anyone's feelings they asked Madame Gosselin to choose someone.

"We'll do a random drawing among the girls present at the time," Madame Gosselin exclaimed. It was me who won. I attended the ceremony. I got almost as many compliments as the bride. "She's so beautiful, what you've done is incredible!" Really, I wasn't even present for the drawing. I suspect the girls, Madame Gosselin included, chose to give me this gift...

MARIE-PIERRE TSCHANN

INTERNIST

For two months, we've had a male nurse with us. He's the first one in the unit in four years. On the other hand, I've never heard of a male nursing aide. Yes, we're only women. Besides a doctor and a few non-resident students and porters who pass through, we're only women here. It's a cultural thing, I suppose. Since the dawn of time, it's been women, midwives, who assist and accompany at the moment of birth. So, symmetrically, it's women who assist and accompany at the moment of death. That must sort out a fair number of things for the men.

When I was a little girl, my mother used to say that men were more impressed by pain. I've heard similar arguments used to justify there being no men in the sector — that as nurses they prefer working in sectors that are supposedly "more physical": the operating room, the emergency department, the recovery ward. I've heard it said that male doctors privilege the search for tangible solutions, that they prefer it to the task of relieving pain, which would explain why, in our unit, the majority of doctors are women.

It's the same thing with resistance to pain. My mother said women can bear more of it. She would say that, proud to have had six children without epidural, when she teased my father: "You men…"

All of that, for me, is just clichés. And clichés, you know, are quick to crumble in the face of disease. In the face of agony.

Sometimes patients confide in us about things they don't dare tell their family. Or things they don't want to tell them, in order to protect them.

I still remember this young woman. Let's call her Aude.

Aude is married to a young man, very nice, very handsome, it must be said. He spends every other night with her, in her room. All of this happens, of course, on a night when the husband isn't beside her. It's a particularly hectic night. One patient screams out in pain, another struggles with insomnia. There's a series of telephone calls. Finally, around two in the morning, things calm down. That's when the light goes on and the beep-beep of Aude's room can be heard.

"I'll go," says Micheline.

"No, let me do it," I say to her.

I go and I find Aude in tears, devastated.

"He'll be with another woman, I know it, one day when I'm not here anymore... I can't bear the idea. I keep trying to think of something else, but I can't, I can't... And I get angry at him, and I feel like a monster. A monster."

I don't say anything. Nothing I could say will calm her down. So I simply take Aude in my arms. I hold her gently. But deep down, in spite of myself, I think that she's right. Her husband will be with another woman. I think it with such coldness that I also feel like a monster.

CHARLOTTE BOUILLON

NURSE

Aurore, the new patient, was thirty-two years old, just like me. She was so young. It was shattering. She seemed even younger than me, maybe because of her pallor and her terribly thin body, weakened by illness. I looked at her file: she was born two months after me. Now, I was born prematurely, at seven months; it's a tradition in my family, most of the women were premature. I couldn't keep myself from believing that deep down we were exactly the same age, give or take a day. A bit of a dangerous idea... I know. You have to steel yourself when you do this job, you have to know how to protect yourself. But the vision of Aurore and her husband, always a bit badly shaven, and her helpless parents, all of it seemed to me so painful, so striking, so unfair.

One day I came into Aurore's room and saw some new faces. Since the beginning, Aurore had only been surrounded by her husband and her parents. This time there were a dozen or so people. Friends, it was easy enough to tell. Young, too, uncomfortable in the room. "They won't come back," I said to myself, "except one or two." Over time, it gets easy to guess what visitors think, to anticipate the recurring situations. Before I left, I took a quick look in Aurore's direction. She seemed too tired to follow the conversation weaving around her room.

A few weeks later, I reluctantly took a vacation. My husband was surprised by my lack of enthusiasm for this trip we had planned with so much excitement and care. I didn't dare tell him how difficult it was for me to leave Aurore... I didn't dare tell anyone. Until Valérie Le Panno, who knows me so well and who had been following my relationship with Aurore since the beginning, guessed everything.

Eventually I talked about it with our psychologist, who told me that my difficulty leaving the hospital showed the degree to which I needed time off. That was indisputable, and very easy to say, but it wasn't easy to do, no...

Before I left, I asked Valérie Le Panno to swear that if something serious happened to Aurore, she would send me a message. I knew perfectly well that in reality we're not allowed to do that, that I was asking her to violate the rules. She looked at me silently and answered that she couldn't promise me such a thing. I was furious.

The third day of our trip, I finally admitted to my husband why I had shown so little enthusiasm before our vacation, and I felt relieved... The two or three next days, I realized that I was finally beginning to enjoy my free time. The weather was beautiful. I was sleeping well. I had started to read a novel my husband had given me. We were eating at a different restaurant every night. At that moment I received Valérie's message. Aurore had just died. I was doubly shocked. By the sad news, but also by seeing, in the middle of my time off, more than a thousand kilometers from the UHC, the weight of Aurore's death diminishing for me, by seeing that I was taking stock of her real importance in my life, just as I had felt a week earlier, the moment the airplane took off, that everything on the ground was becoming tinier and tinier, almost unfamiliar.

In spite of this feeling, Valérie's message ruined my vacation. I had been furious at her because she didn't want to inform me of Aurora's passing. Now I was furious because she had.

HERVÉ MONTEROLIER

NURSE

I'm the only man on the unit. The only male nurse, I mean. There are also a few doctors, but not many. There's still Patrick, Christophe, Olivier, and the other porters. But I'm the only nurse. And I think the perspective of a male nurse is important. We necessarily examine and feel things differently. Now, patients of either sex are so used to seeing women among the nursing aides and nurses that they address me, invariably, as "doctor, doctor." At first I used to blush, embarrassed. At this point I just smile, and sometimes I don't correct them. They seem so happy to have a visit from a doctor.

Five or six days after his arrival, the patient murmured bitterly in front of Danièle and me: "It's too bad, you know, in a week my wife and I will celebrate our silver anniversary. Twenty-five years of marriage... Alas..." And he added that a few months earlier he had planned a surprise dinner for the occasion, before getting his own devastating surprise of the diagnosis and his hospitalization.

Without delay, Danièle, Charlotte, Marie, and I set to work organizing a romantic dinner. The man suspected something was up; his wife, nothing at all.

We chose the family room. We bought candles. We asked the patient what his wife's favorite dishes were. Everything was going smoothly, with this bittersweet joy that spreads through our unit more often than people imagine. It was going to be a lovely evening.

Everything was ready when suddenly the patient's state deteriorated. He didn't have the strength to stand up, not even for a few seconds to plop himself down into a wheelchair. "We'll bring him in his bed," Charlotte decided. The patient shook his head no. This was not how he had envisioned his silver anniversary.

Soon his wife figured out that we were planning something.

"Okay, we'll tell you everything," Danièle relented.

Thirty minutes later, they were seated at the table. The candlelight highlighted the sick man's emaciated face. Neither of the two was hungry. But they seemed enchanted to be there, across from each other, together. They laughed, sadly, at the scene they had played in the hall, commanding the attention and encouragement of much of the unit: she had carried him in her arms. He was no more than skin on bones; she was strong and firm.

At the moment they crossed the threshold of the family room, where Charlotte and I had just lit the candles and filled two champagne flutes that they wouldn't touch, I said to myself—this is my simple mind talking—that twenty-five years earlier it was probably she who was in his arms.

CHANTAL ROUYER

DOCTOR

"Docteuse! Docteuse! I need to know something: how many liters of blood are there in the human body?"

His name was José, he came from some country in South America (Peru, I think, or Ecuador), and he was one of those funny and spontaneous patients with the rare knack for making doctors laugh. Everyone liked his affable face, his mestizo nose, his very black and very close-set little eyes, and most of all his way of speaking French as though he were singing.

José had been living in France for a dozen years or so. An economic migrant, he seemed to have a family back at home, in South America. He had come, he explained, to make a big bundle of money before returning home a millionaire. In the few months he had been living at the hospital, he modified this story from time to time. Sometimes he claimed he had come to marry a French woman and that things had turned sour a week before their wedding. Other times he spoke of himself as a political exile. In any case, it was clear that he worked in building renovation and that he lived in a situation of great precarity.

José had been in the unit for more than a week. He had blood cancer. He bled a lot. He suffered from heavy anemia. His intensive treatment turned his body into a time bomb. In spite of it all, he claimed to be confident and maintained a stoic expression, belied by his grimaces and his forehead roiled with fear.

"*Docteuse, docteuse!* How many liters of blood?"

He always called me that, even though I told him he should just say *docteur* or, as the case may be, something like *docteure*. He kept doing it anyway.

One day, while I was examining José and reading the results of his latest tests, and confirming to him that his anemia had reached a very high level, the thought of a blood transfusion occurred to me. I would have let the idea pass if not for the fact that two days earlier, in light of his worsening case, Fabienne Vinour had spoken in favor of it.

I went to see José to explain the procedure to him. Everyone agreed that he trusted me more than the other caregivers. In his room, as usual, it smelled like cigarettes. He smoked compulsively in secret, which had not gone unnoticed in the unit; Morgane and Solène regularly confiscated his tobacco, but he continued to get a hold of more. Morgane thought it was through a woman who came to see him every two or three days with packs of Marlboros: a statuesque blonde straight out of an American film from the sixties. Close up, you could see she was a fake blonde and that she was approaching fifty, but she looked "good from a distance," as Solène liked to say, laughing.

When José spoke of this woman he called her "my cousin." For her part, she never called him "my cousin"; she always used the phrase "my friend José," and spent less time by his bedside than she did pacing the hallways.

"I need to talk to you, it's important," she declared every time she came, but she always left too soon — or maybe it was me who took too long, who dodged her without really realizing it.

I explained to José that day that, thanks to the transfusion, he would feel less weak. He responded with an evasive pout, looking discouraged.

Even though the transfusion was a success, the anemia came back soon after. The numbers described a strange curve: on Monday his hemoglobin levels would bottom out, on Tuesday they would be back up, Wednesday they would fall again, and so on.

The cost of a transfusion is so high that I discussed it with Fabienne again and we resolved to wait a bit before arranging another. In the meantime, one morning, while I was looking over his fluctuations, trying to read some secret logic between the lines, I heard footsteps in the hall, on the doctors' side, an area where the families don't usually venture. The door to my office was open and from my chair I saw, a dozen meters away, the silhouette of a brunette looking intently at me.

"I need to talk to you, it's important," she said.

It was the blonde, who now had short dark hair.

"Talk about what?" I finally asked her.

"You don't know? José is worried, very worried, because his visa is expiring soon," she answered, sitting down across from me without waiting for my invitation.

I did know this: José had missed his renewal appointment at the police prefecture because he was already in the hospital; missing the appointment was a grave mistake in José's eyes. He didn't want to end up without valid papers.

The blonde (or rather the ex-blonde) had assured him he didn't have to worry. She had talked about it with a lawyer friend. He just had to present a letter or certificate, fancily signed and stamped by the doctors at the UHC. Our social worker had told him more or less the same thing:

"Nobody is going to expel you from the hospital, José, or from the country. You'll resume the process once you've left here."

This was exactly what he feared the most: never leaving the hospital. Living out the last of his days an undocumented immigrant.

"He thinks he's going to be buried in a mass grave, some kind of pit dug for clandestine immigrants," the false blonde began to explain. "Of course he's exaggerating. It's typical of José to make a big drama out of everything..."

I promised I would talk to him and said I would happily sign the letter for the prefecture. I felt guilty for being unable to imagine why it was so serious, so worrisome, to die with an expired visa.

Three days later, since the anemia was rising again and the hemoglobin was low, Fabienne asked me to do a second transfusion. I went to see José with a pang of fear: the first transfusion had made him extremely anxious. This time, however, he was positively beaming:

"It's a sign! I'm being given a once-in-a-lifetime chance!"

"What are you talking about, José?"

He shook his head several times. He smiled and closed his eyes. Nothing else.

In the days following the transfusion, José was on cloud nine. The cousin had come one afternoon, with her blonde wig again, and, per his request, a notebook and a pen. This was when he began to ask all the questions about blood. "How many liters, *docteuse*?" He spent long intervals with notebook in hand, calculating and recalculating figures.

At first, I thought he had called me without a specific objective, just to exchange a few words and distract himself. "In the body, *docteuse*, how many liters?" and I would answer, "It depends," and he would press, "Depends on what?" I would specify, "It depends on the body, José," and he would observe, "That's not very clear," and I would conclude, "Hold on, I'll be back." I remained vague because I wasn't sure I knew the exact answer. One day I made up an excuse: "I'm being paged, I'm needed in another room," looking at my cell phone. José didn't say anything, but I felt like he could tell I was hesitating. I didn't want to admit it, so I added: "There's a formula, you multiply the weight of the body…" and stopped my sentence there: I mean I left the room, went out the door pretending to know the formula perfectly when in fact I had forgotten it. José said, "A formula, yes, I see." I managed to backpedal: "I'll be right back and then I'll explain it to you."

In the hall, I looked it up on the internet. I found the answer quickly, it was easy, I knew it, it had just slipped my mind, and ten or fifteen minutes later I declared, "So, we adults have between five and six liters of blood in our bodies," and he answered, "And the formula?" and I confirmed, "Ah, yes, the formula: there are seventy cubic centimeters of blood in a kilogram," and since he was looking at me silently I opened the calculator on my phone and added, confidently, "For instance, if you weigh seventy-five kilos, multiplied by seventy, your body contains 5.25 liters of blood."

"So I'm losing lots of things at once while I'm here: my health, my life, my patience, weight, and also blood," he protested.

I sensed a retort was necessary.

"You're forgetting that you're also losing pain."

José gave me an ironic grimace and I was unable to add anything, not even a few comforting words, so I left.

In the following days, I saw that this time José's body was responding well to the transfusion. No drops in hemoglobin. No fever or tremors. That surely explained his better appearance, this kind of euphoria in him. But there was something crazier going on: I know it now, but somehow I could feel it already.

It was José himself who finally told me everything: if the majority of patients see a transfusion as a cure at best and relief at worst, José thought he saw the solution to his anxiety about his visa. The connection? He had done some slightly bizarre calculations and, he said, he was only four or five transfusions away from being 100 percent French by blood.

He was joking, I thought. Or maybe he was delirious. Certainly there was a dark irony in all of this. Dying of fright, he was doing everything in his power to not think about his sickness or his visa: just about dying with his old mestizo veins full of foreign blood.

It was Sylvie who found, in the hours that followed José's death, his notebook full of calculations. The notebook was in the bathroom, in the hole where he hid his tobacco. Mixed in with his calculations was also a kind of journal for three or four pages. I had a chance to take a peek. He spoke harshly of a nurse, a girl who left some time ago now and who, truthfully, I never could stand. He explained how one day this girl made fun of him and his calculations. I saw that José had written in French for these three or four pages, dreadful French, riddled with spelling errors—which meant he wasn't writing it for himself, that these pages were meant for someone else. And who else besides me?

I gave the notebook to the blonde woman the last time she came here, to the UHC. I had her phone number. I sent her an SMS telling her we had found something important. She showed up (with brown hair again), after having responded to me by text: "I need to talk to you." Apparently it was easier for her to change her hair than to find new words.

What did she want this time? She said everything without saying anything. She showed up a bit early and came into my office. I handed her the notebook and she put it in a little backpack (a little girl's backpack, pink and white) and, from the same backpack, but another pocket, she took out a thin laminated rectangle. José's visa. I took the card in my hand and looked at the black and white photo, the mestizo face, the prominent cheekbones. When I tried to hand it back, the woman made a motion to refuse it.

I looked at her, confused.

"What is it?"

With her index finger, with a nail painted in fluorescent red, she pointed under José's first and last name in capital letters, and I read: VALID UNTIL...

And then I understood. The date was precisely the date of José's death. And it's crazy, yes, but you can use the same verb for both situations: *expire.*

PATRICK TOMAS

PORTER

Since I was a kid, I've always loved bats. At seven or eight, I already had a passion for them. What I loved most of all is that they're mammals, but everyone seems to have forgotten. Ask the first person you pass on the street and they'll tell you they're birds, or maybe rodents. This bizarreness still fascinates me.

Of course, I know the reputation you're asking for when you love bats. It's like we function a bit in reverse: we're supposed to like the night more than the day, watch vampire movies, listen to goth-rock, and—I mean, why not?—sleep hanging upside down, that sort of gloomy and macabre stuff. But, as you see, I'm a nice guy, someone who wears his heart on his sleeve, as they say.

First, allow me to point out that I chose this job a bit at random, if randomness exists. I knew Olivier and Christophe and two or three other guys who work here as porters. No, I didn't like the idea of working in a hospital. I'm not very good with dead people, sick people. Nobody likes that, even bat fanatics. I mean, deep down, vampires want to live forever...

The really funny thing, though, is that I discovered that my job maybe has a link to my fondness for bats. We porters are, of course, a bit of a species unto ourselves. But above all, and this is what I wanted to talk about, we see our patients upside down, lying on stretchers: just like bats, who fly with their heads down.

I know, you're going to say I'm reading into it, that I'm jumping to far-fetched conclusions, that I'm oversimplifying. All the same, I encourage you to pick up the handles of a stretcher and meet the eyes of the patient. Sometimes you see them face up, sometimes the other way around.

At first, I was bewitched by this spectacle. Bewitched and disconcerted: I would have a hard time telling whether I was looking at a man of thirty, forty, fifty years old. With their heads upside down, the patients became like a puzzle that was impossible to put back together.

I had a friend in school who could read a book upside down. Here at the UHC, I've learned to tell whether a woman is pretty or not by looking at her from the opposite side. My coworkers know I prefer to take the handles from that end. I've gotten so good at looking at the world that way that they sometimes give me upside-down photos of celebrities or singers or actresses or soccer players to look at, and I can always recognize them at first glance.

I make them laugh when I say that here, at the UHC, is where I got my bat degree.

Sometimes I have little outbursts of sensitivity. I'll have tears in my eyes for hours at a time. My colleagues make fun of me a bit, and as soon as I start crying Charlotte Bouillon calls me Madame Fontaine. Really, though, I've noticed that my emotion can make the other caregivers tear up as well. When I started working here, I criticized myself for it. I considered my tears a professional faux-pas, proof of a lack of maturity.

I know some people who hide their eyes behind a pair of Ray-Bans. Me, I sprinkle my face at the sink and say I've just had a bad cold.

One day, as I was leaving the bathroom, I found myself face to face with the wife of a patient: the wife of a man who, more than the others, had a knack for making my tears flow whenever I saw him in his bed.

I was vexed every time I passed this woman. What must she have thought of me?

That day, in front of the bathroom, my eyes all red, I stammered like I'd been caught doing something wrong. The woman looked at me closely; then she cut me off and told me, with the hint of a smile:

"I've wanted to tell you for a while that I like it when you're like this, on the verge of tears... Yes, it's good to see some emotion in a doctor. It's nice, because it's human. And above all it reassures the families. You see what I mean, don't you?"

The parents of the patient in room 4 want to know, at all costs, things nobody can possibly know. Besides a god. Noémie is bold enough to tell them they should go get some air, get out for a bit, take a little walk in town. "It's nice out. It's springtime, you know." Stunned, the parents stare Noémie up and down, from her head to her toes, as if she's completely insane.

As soon as they walk away from their daughter's room, Noémie notices my surprise. I've just arrived at the unit.

"I know, they thought my advice was absurd," she says. "But sometimes families wear themselves out too early. I've seen some who are overly close to the patient, who never leave him alone. Who smother him. People feel guilty, so they stay twenty-four hours a day, and then the patient also feels guilty, guilty for turning their lives upside down like this, guilty for seeing them here twenty-four hours a day. It's a spiral."

An hour later, the parents of the patient in room 4 are back in the hall, where they're usually pacing back and forth, and in a totally unexpected way they come up to me to tell me they have to leave for a minute. They're whispering, as though to avoid letting

Noémie hear their words. They give me their cell phone number. "Just in case," the mother adds.

After the parents have left, I tell Noémie, who's delighted.

"Not bad, right?"

I agree. In truth, though, it seems like an awfully long time while I wait for them. It would be just terrible if something happened to their daughter at this precise moment.

MIREILLE GOSSELIN

UNIT MANAGER

When I hear that palliative care is the unit where people go before they die, instead of getting huffy, instead of explaining more or less patiently that we also treat pain in cases that don't involve imminent death, instead of that, I answer in the affirmative, I smile my sweetest smile, I say yes, that's right, good point, and then I add that you could in fact make the same claim about all the departments in the hospital, any hospital, because, all told, everything worth calling life is just the set of things we do before we die, isn't it? And that, I can assure you, never fails to make an impression.

I think often, since I started working here, about the appetite for life. For three years I've been coming to play in the unit two or three days a month. Each time with someone different. Sometimes a member of the city's symphony orchestra, in which I'm the first-chair violinist; sometimes a jazz musician, since I'm also involved in that scene. First we play in the family room for the patients who want to hear us, with or without their friends or families. Then we go play in the rooms, only if our presence is requested.

Nine or ten months ago I met a patient, Madame Signy, who I wanted to talk to you about. In her youth, she was a pianist and a music teacher. She never stopped practicing her instrument, and she was a music lover of admirable cultivation and retention. The first time I played for her, she recognized all the classical pieces. "Bach, sonata no. 1, second movement," or "Tchaikovsky, concerto for violin in D major," she would say as she hummed along with long passages.

I had a hard time admitting that Madame Signy was seriously ill. She was thin and frail, no question. But there was a striking joie de vivre in her eyes.

After the first time we met, Madame Signy's husband told me privately that she waited eagerly for each one of our visits, and that she had expressed a desire to him: she wanted us to come play until the last moments of her life. She was imagining her death in the unit. She saw herself in her final agonies with us at her side, playing works by Schubert and Haydn.

This was the first time anyone had asked me such a thing. I didn't know how to respond. I couldn't accept on behalf of my companions. I could only accept personally. But accepting meant being called for an emergency, at any hour of any day, to come with violin in hand to the bedside of a dying woman.

To get off the hook, I told Monsieur Signy that I didn't know whether the service would allow such a thing... Knowing Madame Gosselin as I knew her, I assumed the unit would agree to the request. But I bought myself some time.

Before giving my answer, I talked to Madame Gosselin, who gave her approval. Monsieur Signy continued to await each of my visits anxiously. But the illness was devouring his wife. At first, she talked to me passionately about her favorite quartets: Beethoven's last ones (especially the thirteenth and fourteenth), Alban Berg's opus 3, all of Darius Milhaud's quartets, the very first by Samuel Barber (which is where his famous *Adagio* comes from) and Leoš Janáček's *Kreutzer Sonata*, for instance. It was wonderful to talk about these pieces with her. However, bit by bit, her fervor seemed to dull.

Monsieur Signy made a superhuman effort to bring his wife a bit of lightness. And I, too, played with a bit more ardor than usual.

I nearly even overplayed, which had the unfortunate consequence of creating the opposite reaction in such a sensitive music lover.

I'll never forget the case of Madame Signy. In the four weeks leading up to her death, she didn't want to hear anything about me, or my violin, or music in general. She had lost all appetite for the greatest passion of her life. At first, Monsieur Signy and I thought she was feeling rage or disgust, that it was a feeling that would pass. But the most shocking thing was to see her go from that first reaction to complete indifference. One month earlier, she and her husband had made a list of the pieces I would play during her last moments. It didn't include anything mournful. No requiems, quite the opposite: excerpts from Schubert's trio no. 2 and Haydn's last violin concerto.

During the four weeks that followed, I thought a lot about the pieces they had chosen, which I had to adapt to play as solos. I wanted to play flawlessly for her. But above all I wondered about the hidden meanings in her choices. Why, out of all the music in the world, had she opted for those two pieces?

Madame Signy died on a Sunday morning and nobody called me to play during her final throes. She had told her husband that, upon reflection, she wanted only silence at the moment of her passing. Silence and his presence, also silent if possible. When I learned this, I was hurt. I told myself that Monsieur Signy could have at least called me to play the agreed-upon program at his wife's grave. But that was idiotic and petty. In the midst of his pain, Monsieur Signy hadn't had time to think of me.

It's funny, but last week I got an offer to play Schubert's trio no. 2 in public. I accepted without hesitation. And I thought, naturally, about Madame Signy. If you want to come hear me, I'd be truly delighted. It'll be in September, at the Rouen Opera. I'll be playing in homage to Madame Signy. And you can come listen to the music in her honor.

ADÈLE BLANQUI

INTERNIST

The most painful thing, for me, is an empty room. It only happens occasionally: a room stays unoccupied for one or two days, never more. And without a patient, it becomes a dead person's room.

I have a hard time walking into these empty rooms. They remind me not only of the last patient, but also of all the others who have passed on in that bed. All the deaths there have been between these walls.

Once I read this sentence in a book: "It's not death but dead people that make us afraid." It comes back to me every time there's an empty room.

NELLY JUNDZILL

DOCTOR

Never in my life had I seen twin brothers who looked so much alike. They were familiar figures at the hospital; they belonged to the very small circle of patients whose names are known to a good portion of the medical staff. To enter that category in an establishment that several hundreds of patients pass through each day, it's practically mandatory to have some exceptional characteristic. The Descotte brothers, both in their sixties, were not only wonders of nature, they were also extraordinary hypochondriacs. Both single, they lived together, a few minutes from here, and they were inseparable. Each of them came regularly to be checked out for his own problems (most of them imaginary) and also accompanied his brother on hundreds of appointments for issues that generally existed only in his mind.

The Descotte brothers were also in the habit of having a café gourmand, every weekday afternoon, in the cafeteria. You could say they spent more than half of their life in the hospital.

It was at one of those little cafeteria tables that I saw them up close for the first time. They would stay there for hours, silent and pensive. The cafeteria, as you know, is divided into two areas and, by a sort of unspoken accord, those who work at the hospital occupy one and visitors sit in the other. The Descotte brothers, however, preferred the former.

One day, one of the brothers was diagnosed with an incurable disease. Until then, the doctors had been cagey with these Descotte hypochondriacs. Now they were establishing a genuine fondness.

Nothing changed in terms of the brothers' routine. They continued to spend hours at the hospital, drinking their coffee among the doctors. Nonetheless, for the first time, we saw a difference between them. They were no longer 100 percent identical. It was a subtle distinction, yes, but everyone saw it. Everyone could now tell them apart; everyone could tell which one of them was the sick one.

Of course, the other brother immediately began claiming he was gravely ill as well. Hypochondria can be strangely contagious... And he insisted so much that a doctor finally assured him: "Okay, to set your mind at ease, we'll run some tests." It turned out there was nothing, besides a marginally low white blood cell count.

A bit later, the brother who was really sick, Antoine, came to spend a week in the unit. It had been two or three months since I had seen the Descottes. I felt a little pang in my heart to see not just the sick brother so thin and weak but also the other one, Frédéric, in the same condition. They seemed to hold each other up, in the most precarious kind of equilibrium.

My colleagues thought, as I did, that Frédéric was imitating his brother. We assumed he had stopped eating, that he was doing everything he could to keep looking like Antoine. Out of pity? Out of a troubling need to preserve their similarity? Who knows?

So we decided to talk to Frédéric. Antoine was entering a critical phase and would need his brother to be at full strength. Frédéric listened to us indulgently, but with a skeptical curl in his lip. Finally, he began to speak, very slowly, as though explaining something very complex to a group of five-year-olds:

"Our path…"

He paused, with an enigmatic look, before adding:

"… is a single path."

It wasn't all that enigmatic, in truth. He wanted to tell us, basically, that all he and Antoine knew was this double life they had been leading in concert since forever. While his brother was afraid to suffer or die, he was afraid to be alone. Without his other half, as it were.

Obviously we can use the same phrases, word for word, to speak of couples put in a similar position. But the Descotte brothers' symbiosis surpassed anything we had ever seen.

How do you think the story ends? Go ahead, you're the writer! Did they both die at the same time, the invalid and the imaginary invalid? Did Frédéric die first, somewhat egotistically? Okay, I'll tell you: Frédéric practically lived in the unit, always by his brother's side. He stayed day and night. He didn't even want to go home to shower, so sometimes we made an exception and let him use the one reserved for staff.

One day, they requested a leave. It was bizarre, but they spoke in first person plural. Why not? we said, given Antoine's more or less stable state in spite of his fragility. They'd spend four or five days at home. From time to time we'd send a mobile unit, and we'd follow Antoine's progress very closely.

One morning... Yes, I can see you're guessing the end... One morning the mobile unit showed up. It was Joséphine and a girl who no longer works here, a certain Béatrice, I remember it like it was yesterday. They rang the doorbell. Two, three, four times. No answer. They found them dead, both brothers. A doctor came. They tried to estimate the time of death. No, it wasn't a suicide. But they departed together. In the same way I like to think of them arriving in our cafeteria, coordinating the movements of their legs, the swinging of their arms, like soldiers in a parade. Like they were part of an army, of which they were the only members.

CÉCILE MILLIOT

NURSE

I could sense that this woman was waiting for something, or rather someone. Not that she wasn't surrounded. Quite the contrary. Her second husband, her daughter from this second marriage (fairly old, with an even older husband and two teenagers), her son also from the second marriage, a girlfriend, and an old pair of male friends regularly came to visit her. But this woman seemed to be looking over everyone's shoulder, unsatisfied with the presences in front of her, waiting for something extra, something whose absence in that moment seemed to sadden her, obsess her.

We took great pains to calm her and try to understand her anxiety. On days when she was doing better, she sat up straight in her bed, put a handkerchief on her head, tied it under her chin, and looked intently at the door. The other days she was more and more apathetic, her face pallid, white as a sheet of paper, and spent hours on end without a single movement, always attentive to the door to her room.

Through a friend of hers — an old classmate, younger than her — I heard for the first time about her other son: the only child from her first marriage. With an air of both recklessness and sorrow, the old friend told me that this son lived very far away, in Toronto.

So I got the idea of alluding to this son's existence in the presence of the other children. Quite audacious, I know. But it was less risky than doing it directly in front of the mother.

A few days later, I knew everything. The son from the second marriage, Étienne, had sent a message to his half-brother in Toronto to tell him that his dying mother wanted to see him again at all costs. We waited for some reaction from him, some response— a simple "no thank you," at least. But nothing.

I kept my ear to the ground for any news from him. But I still didn't say anything about it to the patient. Until one day when I was getting ready to leave her room, leaving her alone, and she asked me in a low voice, without looking me in the eye, if I had heard from her son. "From Étienne?" I said, as though no other son existed. Or, more precisely, as though I hadn't been informed of his existence. "No, of course not!" she cried, despondent. And after a long sob, she revealed the whole story and told me she no longer had the strength to wait for her eldest son. But she continued to, holding death at bay, drowsing for hours and hours.

The next day, I repeated this conversation to Madame Gosselin, and she called Madame Terwilliger to join us.

"Expectations have a direct influence on the length and the quality of a patient's last days of life," is more or less what our psychologist said.

And it was true: the mother was making such an effort to prolong her life, convinced that her son was coming soon, that her agony was heartbreaking to watch.

I suddenly felt a great bitterness toward this man who would not come to his mother's side, in spite of the searches and the repeated calls from his half-siblings.

The lady died without seeing her son again and without hearing from him. Convinced he had been in an accident or met some other grave fate, or else he would have been there with her.

I hadn't forgotten this episode (not that I could have) when, almost a year after this woman's death, a man in his sixties showed up in the unit one Friday morning. It was the son from Toronto. He wanted to see the place where his mother had died. He wanted to talk to one of us and hear about her last days.

Everyone turned toward me. I had been, certainly, the one who was closest to her.

I invited the man to have a coffee with us, in the family room. There were three of us, if I recall correctly, Danièle, Valentine, and me. His mother's room was occupied, but he agreed to see another one where a man had just died. He spent a few minutes there without saying anything. He looked at the bed, chewing on his lower lip. After which he asked me, in front of my colleagues, in too brusque and imperative a manner:

"Can we talk for a minute?"

I didn't want to talk to this man. I didn't like the way he rubbed his hands together incessantly, as though he was in a hurry. I couldn't stop myself from thinking of the old woman's suffering.

Still, I was curious: why hadn't he come to say goodbye to his mother?

In that instant, I had a bit of a strange idea...

"Okay, we can go to the courtyard for a moment," I suggested.

And, once there, after letting the son talk, after responding vaguely to some of his questions, I murmured, with a hint of shyness:

"Actually... I have something to admit to you."

He made a gesture.

"Go ahead."

"I told your mother, two days before she died, that I had spoken to you."

"You... what?"

We had stopped, both of us, in the middle of the courtyard, among the cars. It was a nice day and the sun, reflected in the windows and on the cars, was in our eyes.

"She needed to hear it. She was so anguished to not have heard from you... She couldn't understand or accept your absence."

I was improvising, not without cruelty. I couldn't help it...

"But... what did you tell her?"

"That we had spoken briefly. That you had called the hospital. Nothing more, really..."

"And she believed you?"

"She needed to believe me. And I think that yes, she believed me."

Her son, too, needed to believe me. But unlike his mother in my made-up story, he wasn't too happy with what I had told him.

So I got scared and told myself I had made a mistake. The son was going to go complain to Madame Gosselin, woe was me! He seemed truly angry, even though he was rubbing his hands together again in an effort to calm himself down.

"I'm sorry," I said politely.

Truthfully, though, I was enchanted by this absurd revenge, because I could see how guilty he felt.

This is the moment, I thought, seeing him so vulnerable. This is the moment to ask him why he didn't come to his mother's side.

And then I made a mistake. I let him speak first.

"I think I need some time to process all this," he muttered. "I'm going to take a walk and I'll be back."

"Of course, I understand," I said.

But I already knew he would never come back.

"Thank you, mademoiselle," he said, shaking my hand.

I could have asked him the question as he walked away through the courtyard. But he never would have answered. My vindictiveness had been stronger than my curiosity.

I have a very simple method for measuring my stress and exhaustion: when the beep-beep of the call bell irritates me to the point of driving me crazy, it means I can't take it anymore. Of course, it doesn't just depend on me. During some periods, we receive three or four patients at the same time who are very demanding, so the bell rings endlessly. It's difficult, I'll admit, when a patient calls you ten times in a row in the space of an hour but doesn't have anything concrete to ask of you. You try to smile, to ask questions: "Yes, madame, yes, monsieur, what can I do for you?" and sometimes they don't do anything but gaze at you, mouth open, happy to see someone looking in on them. You've heard the bell, right? It's shrill, piercing like a syringe... Sometimes I hear it in my car when I'm going home. Sometimes I hear it in the shower. Sometimes I dream about it. Beep beep beep. The bell. Last week, I had a nightmare: the unit was completely empty, all the beds unoccupied, nobody in the halls, I was alone, all alone, but I heard the bell and I opened and opened the doors, in vain... I told my husband about it at breakfast. "I think, Solène," he said, "it's time to take a vacation."

I remember perfectly the day she arrived. She seemed to me quite charming and refined. I even thought her face looked familiar. Nothing more than that... She had already been in the unit for five weeks when rumors started circulating that she had been a fairly famous actress in the fifties, in her early youth.

She was a widow and had kept her married name. In her personal file, she had also put down her maiden name. But she had a third name, her stage name of yesteryear, from half a century earlier. And that name she hadn't written down.

Her past was, nonetheless, known to all (Cécile Milliot had had the audacity to ask her to confirm the rumor) when one evening something unusual happened: a nursing aide from the emergency department came to tell me they had just admitted a man who wouldn't stop talking about our patient.

It was raining cats and dogs that night. The nurse told me they had found the man (an old man) an hour earlier in front of the main train station. He was lying on the ground with a bouquet of flowers and complaining of pains. He had slipped and fallen in the station square. He had just come on the train from a faraway city with the intention of visiting the former actress. Someone had called the fire department, and the old man would only agree to be taken to one hospital in the city. The hospital where he had planned to go before the accident.

I thought, logically enough, that he must have been a friend or a family member. I didn't say a word about it to the woman, for fear of worrying her. I couldn't just tell her, "It seems you have a visitor, madame," without telling her why the visitor hadn't come up to see her. What good would it do to bother her with all that?

All the same, I went to see the old man. I was curious. He was drowsing in a room, laid out on the bed, still dressed as he had been when he slipped in front of the station. He wouldn't let go of the flowers. He refused to take his shoes off.

How on earth had he known that the actress was at our hospital? He told me about a fan club. He was still in shock from his accident and, to make things worse, a doctor had just told him that the fall had likely caused a femoral neck fracture, often mistakenly called a hip fracture. Nonetheless, naturally talkative, the man told me that the fan club had gotten older and its membership had shrunk, to the point that since January there were only two members: a woman who lived in Nice, and him.

That woman had told him about the hospitalization. And he had embarked on a train trip from Limoges, where he lived, to see how she was doing and to realize his whole life's dream: to place a bouquet of roses in the hands of his idol and at last find out the color of her eyes, eyes he had gazed at in black and white, filled with wonder, in a cinema of his youth.

As soon as the man understood that I was an internist in the palliative care unit, he bombarded me with questions. Did I realize what a privilege it was to be at this lady's bedside? And her? How was she feeling? What was she like? What was she saying? What was she doing?

In one of his pockets, the man had two photos of our patient from the time when she was a rising star at Pathé studios. I looked at them in astonishment. Now I too felt the desire to place a bouquet in her hands. And I thought of Valentine Langer, who said we should always have old photos of our oldest patients, to see beyond their most recent mask.

I left the old man reluctantly. I had to get back to my unit. And of course, after the staff meeting, I went straight to the actress's room. I saw her now in a different light. And I couldn't stop myself from telling her that an admirer wanted to meet her. Her reaction then was very feminine: she sent me to get a mirror, she spent five minutes looking at herself and arranging a few locks of her hair, and finally she told me she wasn't presentable, that her admirer would surely be disappointed to see her like this. What did I think?

Three hours later, I was preparing to finish my rounds. My night relief team had just arrived. I think it was Morgane Bruckner and Carine Le Brun. We were going to go over the day's notes, room by room, patient by patient, when I received a call from the emergency department. The old man had finally agreed to take his shoes off, to get in bed under the covers, to put the roses in a vase, to sleep for a bit. And there, against all expectation, in the middle of his sleep, he had simply stopped breathing. He had died ten minutes ago.

I didn't tell the former actress any of this. I went home. I looked up the fan club online. Not a trace. It was a truly secret society.

The next day, when I arrived at the hospital, Amandine d'Avray told me someone had left a bouquet of flowers for me. I understood right away, before reading the little note left by my colleague in the emergency department, that they were the admirer's roses. The bouquet was in a pitiful state. So I went out quickly and bought another. A few minutes later, I placed the roses into the hands of my patient. I didn't tell her the whole truth, I don't know why. I told her the man had departed (an intentionally ambiguous expression) after leaving her this bouquet.

It wasn't too late to realize the old man's wish, even if the flowers weren't the original roses. It was too late, on the other hand, to tell the admirer that the former actress's eyes were emerald green, still luminous, especially when they beheld the bouquet.

My younger brother wanted to be a writer, like you. But he died very young, at twenty-three. He managed to write some poems, two or three stories, and the outline of a novel, that's it. My father was a doctor, just like me, my older brother, and my grandfather. It's a tradition in our family. My younger brother used to say he was the Gustave Flaubert of our family. You know the story of the Flaubert family, right? His father and brother were doctors.

My father, who's still alive, always says it's no use being a doctor if you couldn't save your own son's life. But sometimes we have to accept our powerlessness. And my father, I assure you, knows it perfectly well. I've heard him say more than once that if you can't accept such a thing, then it's best not to devote yourself to medicine.

My brother died twelve years ago. I think of him regularly. Last year we received a patient in the unit who was a nearly perfect copy of my brother at twenty. It was striking for everyone to see such a young patient at a terminal stage. It was even more striking for me, because many times I had the feeling that I was in front of my brother, speaking to him. Even his voice and his way of laughing were similar.

The most ironic thing in all of this is that my brother, shortly before he died, had the following idea for a novel, or rather for a short story: he wanted to write the story of a doctor who, very young (at thirty, let's say), can't save the life of a patient in his sixties. The doctor spends decades with the guilty awareness of having made a mistake, of having been unable to care for this man, until the moment when, as he's nearing fifty, he receives a patient who is physically identical to the patient he couldn't save and who, what's more, is suffering from the same illness.

Of course, I thought of this story when I saw this patient come in. No, he didn't have the same illness that killed my brother. That would have been too much, wouldn't it?

As for my brother, he never wrote that story, but I think it could turn into a good one. You should write it, maybe, if you'll allow me to meddle in your affairs. Yes, you should at least try. I'd be really delighted. So would my whole family, for that matter. Only, if you ever do write it, I'll ask you to give one of the two characters the first and last name of my poor brother. His name was Charles Aurélien Grenon. Don't forget.

MICHELINE ROMÉO

NURSE

This palliative care unit opened on January 20, 2003. Of the nurses and nursing aides from that time, I'm the only one still active in the unit. I'm the doyenne of the service. I'll take my retirement in a few months. I will have served for more than fifteen years in palliative care.

I remember a man born in England. He had lived in France for more than twenty years with his French wife and their children: a sixteen-year-old girl and a boy of eighteen or nineteen. He spoke our language quite well, but he had a strong accent and always mixed up masculine and feminine nouns. He would say *le maladie* and *la cancer*, for instance.

I spoke to him in English. My mother is Irish (she's still alive, she's eighty-four) and I'm bilingual. And for him it was a real pleasure to chat with me in his native tongue. I saw that with his wife and children he mainly spoke French. But I saw, also, that as he got closer to death (he had an incurable cancer) he had to make an extra effort with his French, as if he already had enough work dealing with *son maladie*.

I was fairly young at the time and we were accomplices in a foreign language, and I dare say he even exaggerated his working-class Cockney accent so that our conversations in English would remain truly private, almost secret.

One morning when we were alone, he asked me a favor. He told me about a person in Manchester, his hometown, someone he wanted to inform of the state of his health. After a few weeks of complicity, I knew a bit about his life. He had told me that his only family in England was a younger brother with whom he didn't get along. I immediately thought that this person in Manchester, this someone he had presented without indicating his or her gender, was a woman: an old flame, a mistress, or, why not, an ex-wife. I didn't dare ask him; I figured he would explain it to me one day or another. For the moment, he said only that there was *someone* over there and that he was counting on me for an important mission: to call this person and tell them he was gravely ill in the hospital. He didn't want to do it himself. He couldn't ask such a thing of his wife or of his French family. He had some friends, of course, but not many, and they were really his wife's friends, friends she shared with him.

Ordinarily we refuse to get involved in our patients' private lives. But I said yes. I couldn't refuse. He had made me his Anglophone "anchor" in the midst of his French death.

I think today it would have gone differently: with a simple text message. But this was back when cell phones were still rare. Sometimes I feel a certain nostalgia for those days. I see an old film or

I read an old novel and I think that the story (part of the story, at least) wouldn't be possible today with our mobile phones. As a writer, you must think that too, from time to time. Stories lost forever... unless the author sets them in the past.

My story with the Englishman is part of that past. I never knew the name of the woman to whom my call was destined. I followed my instructions. I called on a Thursday at 10:30 a.m. precisely. I heard a woman's voice say, in English, "You have reached the number..." and nothing else, and I simply said, in my best English, that I had a message "on behalf of Alex, from Fox Street," that he was seriously ill in a hospital in France (no, I wasn't to specify the city or the name of the hospital) and that he was thinking of her during this difficult time in his life. I called from a payphone that's still there, five blocks from the hospital. I asked for a receipt because he wanted to reimburse me for the call, he insisted, and above all he wanted proof that I had made it. He took the receipt in his hands, he looked at it for a long time, like it was a love note or a letter of farewell, or both at once, and finally he murmured: "One minute and twenty-seven seconds..." That was how long my call had lasted, according to the payphone. Such an important piece of news could be told in so little time...

I threw the receipt in the trash, according to his instructions, after telling him I didn't want him to pay me back. But he insisted and insisted. And I saw, from that moment on, that he seemed to let himself go, to give himself up to his cancer.

Two days after he died, his wife came to visit me. I saw her in the hall and I shook with a guilty conscience. She had come back to thank us. And me in particular. I had trouble looking this woman straight in the eye, and yet, at the same time, I had nothing serious to feel sorry for.

Ever since then, I've never told anyone that I made that call. No one except my husband. You're the second person I've poured this all out to. Not to say I don't think about it. On the contrary, I'll remember him always: my English patient. Yes, like the film.

LINDA MOUILLERON

NON-RESIDENT STUDENT

No, I don't talk about the things that happen here in the unit with my friends or family, except with my mother. She's the only one who, two years ago, didn't try to discourage me from going into the service. She's the only one who asks me questions that go beyond the customary generalities. Everyone else asks me almost nothing; everyone else understands nothing. And I think, in fact, that they don't want to understand. Talking about death and suffering isn't within everyone's grasp. So I keep quiet. I protect them.

AMANDINE D'AVRAY

NURSE

There was the mother and there was the daughter. No one else. A little female family. The mother was the patient. The daughter worked all day, came to see her mother for several hours when night fell, and went home fairly late, around 10 p.m., and that's how the days passed, besides the weekends.

After two weeks, the daughter showed up unexpectedly in our little lounge, where we drink coffee and sometimes (I must admit) smoke a cigarette, to relax, especially when there's been a death, despite the rule against smoking in the building. The daughter showed up and asked us:

"I was thinking about something last night. What is, in your opinion, the mistake families make most often with patients?"

There were three of us that day, Micheline, Isabelle, and me. This was the first time the relative of a patient had asked me a question like that.

Isabelle remained silent. Me too. Then, all of a sudden, Micheline started to speak in a voice that was both serious and tender:

"You know you can stay and sleep here, if you want? I'm telling you because I see, fairly often, that families spend the night with the patients only at the end, when they're already in a very fragile state or almost unconscious. It's a shame, because you have to talk to each other, to say goodbye, and nighttime is ideal for that... You should spend a few nights here, with your mother."

At these words, with a voice slightly choked by emotion, the daughter humbly responded, "Thank you," and left.

Micheline left almost right away, while Isabelle and I stayed silent. One or two minutes later I heard Isabelle's voice, almost as though from far away:

"Shit! I should have asked that when I was fifteen and I was in the hospital with my mother..."

I approached her and put a hand on her shoulder. Isabelle smelled like coffee and her eyes were puffy with tears. My own pain rose to the surface and, for fear of starting to cry, I made some excuse and left.

When night came, I thought that Isabelle should have asked that question, yes. But that wasn't enough. She would have had to find someone like Micheline. If she had asked that question of someone like me, I would have been incapable of giving her such a simple, such a sensible piece of advice.

YVONNE-FÉLICE GUIRAUD
MOBILE UNIT NURSE

I was brand new to the unit. I had just said something stupid to a patient.

"You're too young, that's your problem!" she had grumbled. "In twenty years you'll get it. Now leave me alone and come back in twenty years. I might not still be here..."

Too young? Certainly not, I should have said. Sure, I looked like a little girl, but I felt quite mature for my twenty-five years.

I went home furious. For the first time in my life, I hated a patient. I had a terrible weekend. I talked about the incident to my mother, my friends, my boyfriend at the time.

In the end, I prepared a long speech to deliver to this woman. I even wrote down some sentences that I rehearsed on the bus to the hospital on Monday morning. Only the woman had died on Sunday night.

Nobody at the UHC knew about the incident. But when I got home, I was unable to admit that the woman had died while I was speaking scornfully of her. I didn't have the strength to say it. I barely had the strength to say that in the end I hadn't given my spiel. That it hadn't been worth the trouble.

All the patients in the department have something to resolve
before dying. They want to let go of a more or less explosive secret,
express a regret or a final wish, see someone again or bring up a
specific memory, understand a particular thing, relive and retell
for the nth time, but also for the last time, you never know, a very
intense experience that they once had, that they saw, that they
lived through... Yesterday morning, for instance, a patient called
me in to discuss his funeral in detail. Ordinarily it's the family who
comes to find me to discuss this problem. The relatives sometimes
ask if I have any ideas, and the question goes beyond just my point
of view, they want to know if I'm aware of the patient's wishes, it's
so uncomfortable and painful for them to discuss it with him, they
can't do it, they can't bring themselves to talk about death. At the
same time, I often see patients who want to arrange everything to
make sure their wishes are respected (burial, cremation, destina-
tion of the ashes), to anticipate the concerns and the procedures,
or because they need to talk about it, because taking care of their
funeral allows them to prepare themselves a bit more to face death,
if in any case we agree that there's such a thing as being prepared

to face death. Yes, it's difficult, very difficult. Patients, in spite of their courage, rarely use words like *death* or *dying* or *deceased*. Over time, I've found a euphemism: I talk with them about *the next step*.

My presence, as the only social worker in the department, is requested, for example, when there's a conflict in the family: a mother who's lost all contact with the father of her children and who is concerned about their future after she passes; brothers and sisters in dispute while their father or their mother lays dying. Most often, I discover that the situation is much more complex and convoluted than it appears at first glance. I remember a man in his thirties. He was surrounded by his parents and his sister, an older sister with a strong personality. His partner was also present: a man who was younger and whose origins were more modest. The patient's family had known for two years that he was homosexual and living with another man. But knowing something doesn't mean you accept it. Relations between the family and the partner were hardly cordial. Even worse, they seemed to be entering a phase of mutual rigidity and mistrust. Finally, the patient asked if I could come by to see him. And he arranged to see me by himself. He was weaker than ever; his face had turned ashen and he seemed in great pain. I quickly understood what he had to resolve before departing: he was afraid that his family, after his death, would cut out his partner. He wanted to leave him not only his little studio downtown, where they tended to stay, but also a sum of money he had taken care to save. But he was in a delicate position, legally speaking. They had talked about this with friends. Now, upon reflection, he and his partner were thinking of entering a civil union, and he was thinking of drafting a will too. He wanted my opinion and my help. I told him that if that was what he wanted, then it was the best course of action to take, and that I was authorized to call in a notary.

It was a strange ceremony. The parents and the sister stayed off to the side, unsmiling, looking mournful and a little outraged. It was like they were there not to share an important moment, a moment of joy, but to be witnesses to these two changes they could barely accept. Suzanne Daviel came two hours before everyone else to make up the patient. It was Clémence who had the idea, and happily Suzanne was available. A woman in another room had a makeup kit full of products, and our beautician did such a magnificent, miraculous job that he absolutely didn't look sick at all. He looked like a movie actor. For my part, I had explained everything to the notary, whom I know well, and he had wanted to celebrate both things at once, or rather one after another, except that the patient had had the idea (rather poetic, if you ask me) to begin with the will and end with the civil union, in order not to end on the darkest note, the most macabre.

Would you believe me if I told you the patient died a few hours later? No sooner had the guests left than he had a light dinner, said to his partner, who was alone by his bedside, "I'm sleepy, I need to lie down," and he never woke up. He had resolved his issue and was ready to leave. He died impeccably made up... I think often about that detail.

LOU VILLARSON
DOCTOR

Most of my friends and acquaintances have never seen a single dead person in their entire life. We're a long way from the time when grandparents died at home. Such a long way that we're disoriented, lost, in the face of death.

In a similar way, the medical industry and very powerful antibiotics have erased pain almost entirely. We no longer experience great pain, except in certain end-of-life cases, when morphine and its equivalents can no longer relieve it.

I discuss this often with the other doctors. A department head, a man I find quite sensible, likes to say that "awareness of death changes the flow of time." I sometimes wonder if you can have a complete awareness of life without any, or almost any, awareness of death, of pain. What do you think of that idea? I know, I know, I have an obsession with asking myself impossible questions...

I've just come back to the unit after four months off. I underwent a very delicate operation. In fact, I nearly died. But here I am, back again. Of those four months, I spent two in the hospital. Another hospital in this city. Not this one, no. I didn't want to be here, even though I know many people in other departments. Or, rather, for that reason. I wanted to be at ease. I wanted to be anonymous. Yes, I know, being anonymous is a fantasy. No one is ever anonymous. What I mean is I wanted to be just a patient. Mostly I didn't want the nursing aides from the other hospital to know that I'm also a nursing aide. That was my humble idea of anonymity. Unfortunately I planned the whole thing poorly. I should have told my friends here to keep my secret, though asking them that would be tantamount to ordering them not to breathe, or to become someone else. The fact is that after the operation, when I woke up from my intense anesthetic sleep, the news had spread like wildfire and all the nursing aides already knew I was a colleague.

I won't say they changed the way they addressed me or cared for me. It was me who changed towards them. It was me who was embarrassed. When a nursing aide would say she was going to bathe me, I'd say, "No no, I can do it." And I tried, yes, I really tried. But it was impossible: I couldn't do it, I was weak, I was in pain, and that put me even more ill at ease.

I underwent two operations, to be exact. Or, to be even more precise, one operation in two stages, a kind of drama in two acts. For once, I found myself at the center of the action. I almost died, truly. In another hospital. But here I am, back again. It's like a resurrection. It's like a second life, even professionally speaking. After what I've been through, I look at my work differently, I look differently at patients and families and the hospital and the doctors... I look at everything, not without perplexity, and I have the vague feeling—no, those aren't the right words, I have the very painful certainty that I've just been fooling around until now. That I've gotten it all wrong. All wrong.

I'm exaggerating, I know, but after my experience I've been thinking that such a thing should be mandatory for all of us. Nursing aides, nurses, doctors: we should all be patients, for a month, before coming to work here.

CHRISTOPHE ORSINI

PORTER

It's ridiculous. And it's urgent. Every time we come into the unit to pick up a body, we have to do the strangest, most absurd ballet. Not only do we close the doors, with the help of the nurses and the nursing aides, in the hopes of diverting the attention of the other families and the other patients, while we move the stretcher through the hallway and bring the corpse that we've made invisible — or, really, even more visible under the sheets that are supposed to hide it — not only do we do all that, but then on top of it all there's the problem of the elevator... The hardest thing at any given moment, not just during peak hours, is finding an elevator just for us, I mean finding an empty elevator without coming across a family or another patient. That only happens very rarely. And we can't conceal what's hidden under the sheets, on the stretcher. Which is why every day, when I finish my shift, I think to myself that it's urgent, they need to put in a second elevator.

I have a friend who works in a hotel. She does housekeeping in the mornings, so that the guests who have just arrived and those who are staying at least one more day come back to an impeccable room. She tells me that people leave behind all kinds of things. Sometimes they do so voluntarily (an empty water bottle), sometimes involuntarily; sometimes insignificant objects like an old sock, sometimes valuables.

In the seven years I've worked at the UHC, in this unit the whole time, I think I can say that people never forget anything. As though the families are deathly afraid to do so. As though the nurses and the nursing aides are horrified by the idea of finding the smallest trace, and insist that the families be vigilant. That's maybe the main difference between a hotel and a hospital unit like this one, between a temporary room and a room in which we might die.

You should talk to the workers who do the housekeeping in those units where people rarely die. Do patients often forget things there, like they do in a hotel? I have no idea. My friend tells me she's supposed to turn in what she finds. To management, to the reception desk. I don't know. But from time to time she finds a handsome watch, or a ten-euro bill, things like that, and she keeps them. She's paid very poorly at the hotel, she lives alone with her three kids, and a nice watch allows her to buy a month's groceries at the supermarket, you know as well as I do.

In seven years at the hospital, I have found nothing but an almost empty pack of cigarettes (hidden by a patient from his family, I suppose), an old book with all its pages torn out, one or two bus or train tickets, always expired, and nothing else... Except a little notebook hidden in the bathroom, which Chantal Rouyer surely told you about. I was the one who found the notebook and gave it to her. Nothing else in seven years. A harvest my friend would get in a single day at the hotel.

Instead of abandoned objects, we get visits from families and the presents they give us. As a general rule, they let one or two months go by before they come to thank us and give us something nice: flowers and most of all candy, chocolates, pastries, even homemade cakes made just for us. Usually they give them to the nurses. They let a little bit of time go by. Time to grieve. And never, ever do they want to see the room again. They stay with us in the hallway, in the family room, in the area as close as possible to the exit. They try to smile, to show us they're doing better. They generally turn to face away from the room where their loved one died. And ultimately that's why, I believe, they don't want to forget anything. They want to be done with that room. Anything not to have to go back there.

FABIENNE VINOUR
DOCTOR

Palliative care made me who I am. The road wasn't an easy one, but I'm grateful to this unit. I chose medicine because I wanted to get out of my social situation. When I was very young, still a teenager, one of the first things I told myself was: I need a prestigious job, a job that will allow me to have a house and a nice car… Ten years later, I didn't like the person I was. Ethically speaking, I hadn't become the doctor I wanted to be. I look at myself in retrospect and I see in my behavior a form of maltreatment, a certain absence of humanity. I see individualism, when medical care is collective work.

I like to challenge myself from time to time. It's just part of my personality. Today, I think it's easier to be a good doctor when you're happy and at peace with yourself, when you still feel desire. It's not always easy. Progress is fragile and you tend to harden yourself.

My thirty-year-old daughter is a doctor. That brings us closer together.

I tell her often that others get it wrong when they say a good caregiver needs to find an ideal distance from their patients. I tell her that what we have to find is the ideal presence. And that's far from just a simple play on words.

I also tell her that as soon as I understood that, I became a doctor worthy of the word.

VOLUNTEER SOCIAL WORKER

I saw the ad on a bus. The Association for the Terminally Ill was looking for volunteers to spend time with patients in very fragile health or at the end of their lives. Six years now I've been doing it. I come one day a week, around four or five hours each time, I visit the rooms, I offer my presence, my attention, my company. I always say we're a blank screen, an empty space, or in any case someone anonymous to whom patients can express their doubts, their fears, their memories. If they talk to us about their fear, it's mostly to spare their relatives a bit. Generally, my presence is very welcome. Yes, of course, things aren't always ideal. From time to time someone unleashes their anger on me, but that's quite rare. From time to time a family receives me very cordially and I discover right away that that slightly forced cordiality is really a way to put up a wall between the patient and me; even the arrangement of bodies, all around the bed, hiding the bed, is a method of hiding the patient away, taking them out of the equation, answering for them. In those cases I don't get mad at them; I've learned to be indulgent, to not judge people in difficult circumstances too much.

My friends and relatives often say, "Oh, I admire you! I'd never be able to do something like that." The most curious among them, the most open, want to know what exactly I do when I stay by a sick person's side. "I don't do anything," that's my usual answer, and they look at me dumbfounded. But it's the truth. I don't do anything. I don't follow any plan, I don't make any effort. I sit down next to them, neither too far away nor too close. I'm there. I lend my ear, I joke around or I don't, depending on the case, I nod in agreement or I don't, depending on the case, I commiserate or I don't, depending on the case. I empathize. That above all else: empathy. Sometimes I don't even open my mouth in the half day I spend among the patients. Sometimes no one opens their mouth, and still exchanges of a troubling intensity take place.

The hardest thing, at first, was holding their gaze. Little by little, I learned to do it. I learn unbelievable things from patients. I've learned to touch people, me who's always been a bit cold. I've also learned not to touch them too much, to do with patients what they want me to do and not what I want to do with them.

Just last week — without even looking any further back — I spent fifty minutes next to a very old woman. She looked into my eyes without interruption. I took her hand and we stayed there like that, the two of us, until the moment when she made a discreet and delicate motion, almost invisible, with her mouth. And I understood: that would do. I was to leave her alone again. I stroked her hair, she smiled briefly, and that was it. We stayed silent. A word, a single one, would have ruined everything.

ELSA ALMAKI

NURSE

When Nadia's grandfather arrived as a patient, here in the unit, at first Nadia wanted to take care of him and asked to work in the section of the department that included his room. Nobody objected, but two or three days later Nadia talked to Madame Gosselin, who in turn talked to Madame Terwilliger, and we all gathered for a little meeting, something we call a "mini-staff" here, in order to talk: Nadia was requesting the opposite after all. She had just discovered that she'd made the wrong decision. Wrong for her as a nurse. Wrong for the other patients, because it was impossible for her to look after them with the same devotion she had for her grandfather, to the point that Nadia felt like the other patients no longer existed, like she was neglecting them, scorning them.

Staff meetings are for that purpose, to talk to each other when a problem arises, to think it through together, to look for solutions. Everyone agreed that we would take the opposite approach from the previous one and keep Nadia away from her grandfather's bed. Nonetheless, two days later, she had a new request: she no longer wanted to know or hear anything about her grandfather while she was on the clock. She was stunned to see that even the smallest bit of news about him, even a little comment that made its way to her by accident, had the power to distract her, throw her off course, to the point that she lost track of all her other patients. Her wish wasn't easy to satisfy, since we tend to talk constantly, during our working hours, about each of the sick people. Danièle Pourcely and I came up with a method. Nadia's grandfather was in room 3, which was in our section, while Nadia and her partner at the time were assigned to rooms 7 through 12. To avoid saying the first or last name of Nadia's grandfather in front of her, and also the simple phrase "the patient in room 3," which would also catch her attention, Danièle and I spoke of the "patient in room 2," in reference to the patient in room 2, and of the "patient in 2" to mean the patient in room 3, her grandfather. I'm sure we could have found a better solution, but that's what came to us. Not only was the ruse tricky to put into practice, but it also had its share of risks, because in the first few days I almost gave the "patient in room 2" pills that were meant for the "patient in 2," who was the patient in room 3, if you follow me. Finally, after two days of narrowly avoiding errors and mix-ups, Danièle and I began to get used to it, just like someone learning to use a foreign language, or rather a secret code.

I wonder if Nadia didn't suspect something, hearing us talk almost exclusively about a single patient. Danièle had chosen the man in room 2 because he was what we call a demanding patient. It'd be believable, she thought. But choosing a quiet patient would have been better; the doubling of the rooms would have been less obvious.

Suspicions or not, over the following weeks Nadia was able to forget for a few hours every day that her grandfather was there, barely a few meters away (if you can ever forget a thing like that, if deep down you're not just pretending to forget), and could, as a result, live up to her reputation as an extremely effective nurse.

Nadia has always been a very strong woman, but she was faced with an abnormal situation, because in spite of the information that the whole unit hid from her by way of these complex jugglings, there was also the issue of visits. The closest relatives (Nadia's parents, her sister, her sister's husband) already knew they shouldn't talk to her while she was working, and talk to other nurses instead. But periodically we would see an aunt or a distant cousin arrive and, not knowing what was what, pounce on Nadia to talk to her about the grandfather.

All of this lasted for almost two months, and the situation took on an almost schizophrenic character: Nadia would arrive fifteen or twenty minutes early, in the morning or the afternoon, depending on her hours at the unit, and ask us questions, us, the nurses and nursing aides and doctors, the way close relatives of patients do; after that, she would go put on her scrubs, arrange her hair in a big bun, and all of a sudden she would become a nurse and her grandfather would be taboo. Until the end of the day, when she performed the same metamorphosis in reverse, off with the scrubs, down with the bun, and stayed among us for another half hour, lingering by her grandfather's side (Nadia preferred to see him after work, not before), chatting with her relatives and asking the doctors question after question. It must have been draining for her; at the same time, it was like Nadia had an actress's skill for inhabiting and leaving her character with a certain lightness, and, in between, playing the role to perfection—without the slightest lightness.

The situation had become oddly normal when the grandfather's health gave some alarming signs. One day he had a major attack, a severe hemorrhage. We hadn't talked about what we would do in such a case, but it's true that in these circumstances the borders between sections can get blurry. That's why Nadia suddenly found herself taking care of her grandfather. I think I remember her spending almost an hour at his side, and that she had a hard time going back to work again, to the point that Madame Gosselin suggested Nadia stay by his side; this once, Madame Gosselin would help us with the patients.

This first attack was followed by several others, each more dramatic than the last. After a week, I witnessed one of the most difficult staff meetings in the history of our unit. Nadia's relatives, after a long exchange with the doctors and Madame Terwilliger, had come to us to request a sedation, at the insistent request of the grandfather. In the world of palliative care, two classic situations often lead to a request for sedation: respiratory distress, similar to asphyxiation or suffocation, and hemorrhages we characterize as "cataclysmic." Nadia's grandfather had the latter, accompanied by a sharp, uncontrollable pain.

So you understand the process, the request for sedation is intended to diminish or eliminate a situation that the patient experiences as unbearable. Sometimes it means a temporary sleep. Sometimes the situation is so alarming and so irreversible that it means a permanent sleep. It's not euthanasia, because in active sedation there's no question of desiring or provoking death. And it's a relatively rare measure.

Of course, Nadia knew all of this. She had gone with her relatives when they talked to Madame Terwilliger. She had explained to her own parents that the ideal would be a temporary sedation in which a reversal of the situation is possible and hoped for, but that in point of fact it was necessary to be realistic. She had done all of this in the moments when she was undoing her bun and taking off her scrubs. And now, having become a nurse again, she had the courage to attend the staff meeting and hear what we were saying about her grandfather. Of course, it was more than just simple courage; really, it was an intelligent way to care for him.

Anyway, it had just been explained to us that Nadia's grandfather's request was reasonable, that we were going to go ahead with the sedation, when Nadia raised her hand, like a schoolgirl, and asked to be the nurse in charge: the one who pressed down on the syringe. On the faces of the others I read a mix of surprise and admiration, but also a hint of skepticism, which began to grow in the coming hours. Would she really be able to do it? Or would she change her mind, as she had already done in the beginning with the distribution of rooms? I know Nadia noticed our doubts. And I know she was a little embarrassed when Madame Terwilliger said that of course she had the right to be the nurse in charge, but that she should also feel free to modify her choice.

It was a Tuesday, if I remember correctly. Anyway, let's say it was a Tuesday morning and the sedation was planned for Wednesday.

Nadia confirmed her wish, the same way Nadia's family confirmed their request for sedation. As for the grandfather, he hardly spoke, he was sleeping almost continuously; we had raised his morphine dose but the pain was still there, persistent, and his hemorrhages were multiplying.

A sedation can last several minutes. You can use more than one product, because each organism reacts differently. Let's say that each of us has our weak points and our strong points and that one product doesn't just produce one effect. Nadia's grandfather was no exception. After a first attempt, we had to change the product and then, yes, the real sedation began.

Ordinarily there are three or four of us for a sedation: doctor or internist, nurse, and nursing aide. This time we were six or seven, to be there with Nadia. Ordinarily, all eyes are focused on the patient during the procedure. This time, our attention was split. Me, in any case, I was mostly looking at Nadia, her face tense and vigilant.

In spite of her uncertainties, Nadia kept her composure. It was truly remarkable. From a purely physical standpoint, pressing down on the syringe is a trivial gesture. It takes barely a few seconds. The intense thing, I think, is the moment that follows, the nerve-racking gap between the action and its consequences. In the case of Nadia and her grandfather, I couldn't help thinking the action would have additional consequences, directly for her.

I think Nadia pressed down on the syringe six times total. And I assure you that each time she did she seemed to grow ten years older. Maybe I'm embellishing a bit, but at one point I felt like I was watching an almost alchemical act: the grandfather's face relaxing, easing up, revealing to us like never before inner depths that I wouldn't call youth so much as non-age—and at the same time Nadia's face seeming to age, her skin wrinkling and her eyes veiling over, as though death were spinning a spiderweb around her.

It didn't last more than a moment. I wouldn't be surprised if the other girls told you they didn't see any of this. Me, I saw it. Or I felt it, rather, and that made me see it. Probably. Anyway, it didn't last more than a second, like a mirage. I was devastated, crushed to my core, when Nadia pressed down on the syringe for the last time. At that moment, suddenly, she seemed to get younger again… She made a fatalistic motion with her head, leaned over her grandfather, placed a kiss on his forehead, and then she became the same Nadia as always once again. Except she wasn't the same anymore, that was clear. No, none of us was the same.

THE UNIT